# THE INNOCENT'S SHAMEFUL SECRET

BY
SARA CRAVEN

MILLS & BOON

First Published in Great Britain 2017
By Mills & Boon, an imprint of HarperCollins*Publishers*
1 London Bridge Street, London, SE1 9GF

© 2017 Sara Craven

ISBN: 978-0-263-92424-4

Printed and bound in Spain
by CPI, Barcelona

**There was a violent flash of eerie g . .
light and then, almost at once and right
above their heads, an ominous rumble,
building slowly and inexorably to a
roaring, deafening crash as if the cave
was collapsing on top of them.**

Selena cried out, her voice lost in the uproar, and
stumbled forward, her hands reaching out to Alexis, who
caught her and held her until the last terrifying echoes
of the thunder died away and all she could hear was the
tumultuous thud of her own heartbeat.

And beneath her cheek his—like the relentless rhythm
of a drum.

His hand moved down, impelling her silently to look
up at him. To read his intention in the sudden flare of
his gaze as he bent and his mouth found hers, gently,
sensuously, coaxing her lips to part for him.

She leaned into the heat and strength of his body,
welcoming his kiss, responding with bewildered ardour
as it deepened and a shiver of pleasure feathered
enticingly across her skin.

When, at last, he took his lips slowly from hers she
made a small, lost sound in her throat that never became
an actual word—even if she'd been able to think of one.

She registered that the crackle of the lightning had
become less frequent and the answering thunder had
become a sullen mumble in the distance.

'The sto

There w
contrary

3011780278710 7

# Secret Heirs of Billionaires

*There are some things money can't buy…*

Living life at lightning pace, these magnates are no strangers to stakes at their highest. It seems they've got it all… That is until they find out that there's an unplanned item to add to their list of accomplishments!

Achieved:

1. Successful business empire

2. Beautiful women in their bed

3. *An heir to bear their name…?*

Though every billionaire needs to leave his legacy in safe hands, discovering a secret heir shakes up his carefully orchestrated plan in more ways than one!

Uncover their secrets in:

*Unwrapping the Castelli Secret* by Caitlin Crews

*Brunetti's Secret Son* by Maya Blake

*The Secret to Marrying Marchesi* by Amanda Cinelli

*Demetriou Demands His Child* by Kate Hewitt

*The Desert King's Secret Heir* by Annie West

*The Sheikh's Secret Son* by Maggie Cox

Look out for more stories in the
**Secret Heirs of Billionaires** series, coming soon!

Former journalist **Sara Craven** published her first novel, *Garden of Dreams*, for Mills & Boon in 1975. Apart from writing—naturally!—her passions include reading, bridge, Italian cities, Greek islands, the French language and countryside, and her rescue Jack Russell cross Button. She has appeared on several TV quiz shows, and in 1997 became the champion of UK TV show *Mastermind*. She lives near her family in Warwickshire—Shakespeare country.

### Books by Sara Craven

### Mills & Boon Modern Romance

*Inherited by Her Enemy*
*Seduction Never Lies*
*Count Valieri's Prisoner*
*The Price of Retribution*
*The End of Her Innocence*
*Wife in the Shadows*
*His Untamed Innocent*
*The Innocent's Surrender*
*Ruthless Awakening*
*The Santangeli Marriage*
*One Night with His Virgin Mistress*
*The Virgin's Wedding Night*
*Innocent on Her Wedding Night*
*The Forced Bride*
*Bride of Desire*

### *Seven Sexy Sins*

*The Innocent's Sinful Craving*

### *Men Without Mercy*

*The Highest Stakes of All*

Visit the Author Profile page at millsandboon.co.uk for more titles.

# CHAPTER ONE

SELENA SAW THE letter as soon as she opened the front door, the blue airmail envelope unmissable against the brown matting.

She halted abruptly, recognising the Greek stamp, her stomach lurching as a sudden image blazed into her mind of tall bleached columns rearing into an azure sky, with a pool of grass hidden among the fallen stones at their feet. And the soft murmur of a man's voice in the sunlight, and the brush of hands, lips and warm, naked skin against her own.

She gasped, the plastic carrier bag she was holding slipping from her numb fingers, sending the lemons it contained bouncing and rolling down the narrow hall to the foot of the stairs.

Before she realised almost in the same instant that the untidy scrawl on the envelope could only be Millie's. No one else's. And alarm was replaced by growing anger.

Nearly a year of silence, she thought, her throat muscles tightening. And now—what? Another diatribe of recrimination and accusation with the pen scoring the paper just as her sister's furious voice had scraped across her flinching senses in that last disastrous telephone conversation?

'It's all your fault,' Millie had accused tearfully. 'You were supposed to help—to put things right. Instead you've behaved like a brainless idiot and ruined everything for both of us. I'll never forgive you, never, and I don't want to see you or speak to you again.'

And the phone had gone down with a crash that sounded as if it was in the next room rather than hundreds of miles away in a *taverna* on a remote Greek island.

Leaving her with the knowledge that there was little she could have said in her own defence even if Millie had been prepared to listen. That she had indeed behaved like a fool and worse than a fool.

But she'd suffered for what she'd done in ways that Millie could not even imagine, or was determined to ignore.

Because since that phone call, there'd been nothing. Until now…

She was sorely tempted to leave the letter lying there. To step over it and walk into her living room and begin the new life that had filled her thoughts on the bus journey home.

Except it wouldn't just go away. It wouldn't disintegrate or vanish on a breeze. And, in spite of everything, curiosity would be bound to get the better of her in the end.

She bent stiffly and picked up the envelope, walking through the living room, and tossing it on to the worktop in her small galley kitchen, before filling the kettle and setting it to boil.

She'd originally planned to make a jug of fresh lemonade, clinking with ice, and enjoy it in the warmth of her tiny courtyard. A quiet celebration of this unexpected fresh start.

Now what she needed instead was a caffeine rush, she thought bleakly, taking the jar of coffee and a beaker from the cupboard.

While the kettle was coming to the boil, she went back to the hall, collected the lemons, and put them in the fruit basket.

Idiotic, she told herself, to panic like that. Needless, too. Had she really thought, even for a moment...?

No, she told herself harshly, her hands clenching into fists. You do not—*not*—go there. Not again. Not ever.

She made her coffee strong and carried it outside, settling herself on the elderly wooden bench in the shadiest corner, making herself recap the previous events of the morning and try to recapture something of its optimism.

She had been alone in the classroom, taking down the wall display for Mrs Forbes and putting it in a folder while she considered rather anxiously how she should occupy the unpaid six week summer break ahead of her, when her reverie was interrupted by the arrival of Mrs Smithson, the head teacher.

She said briskly, without preamble, 'Lena, we heard last week that Megan Greig has decided not to return after her maternity leave. Her job as teaching assistant has therefore become a permanent instead of a temporary post, and the staff and governors agree with me that it should be offered to you.' She gave Selena a brief, friendly smile. 'You've worked very hard and become a real member of the team at Barstock Grange. We all want this to continue, especially Mrs Forbes, and hope you do, too.'

'Well—yes.' Selena was aware she must sound dazed, having expected to be once more jobless and probably homeless by Christmas. 'That—that's terrific.'

This time, Mrs Smithson's smile was broader and tinged with relief. 'Then we're all pleased. You'll be sent official confirmation in the next week or so. And—see you next term.'

Selena's state of euphoria had lasted throughout her journey home and the short walk to her tiny terrace property. Until, that was, she'd opened the door...

She didn't need to be subjected to another rant, she thought wearily, or, indeed, to the other possibility—a request to borrow money.

If so, she's going to be disappointed, she told herself, because I'm skint.

Besides, I need to concentrate on my own priorities, like looking for somewhere else to live where children and animals are allowed.

She and Millie had always wanted a pet, she remembered, but Aunt Nora would never agree, clearly believing that two orphaned nieces were sufficient responsibility.

And, considering what had happened, perhaps she'd been right.

Over the years, it had become clear to Selena that

Miss Conway had offered her late sister's children a home more from a sense of duty than any warmer feeling, family visits having been few and far between. But, as she got older, she'd realised that her aunt's decision owed an equal amount to self-interest.

Her valued role as a pillar of local society in Haylesford might have taken a serious knock if word had got out that she'd allowed her nieces to be put into care. A lot of people might have felt that charity should begin at home.

Having experienced it, Selena wasn't so sure. Eleven years old, shocked and wretched with the loss of her parents, killed in a collision with a hit and run driver, it hadn't seemed to matter where she and Millie went, or what happened to them, as long as they were together.

Although they were as different as chalk and cheese, physically as well as temperamentally.

Millie, two years her junior, was a golden girl, small, curvaceous and pretty, her hair a deep, rich blonde which curled slightly. Selena was tall and on the skinny side of slender. Her eyes were grey to Millie's blue, and her skin much paler than her sister's peaches and cream complexion.

But the big difference was her hair, almost at the silver end of the spectrum, and totally straight, spilling halfway down her back, even when confined to the thick braid insisted upon by Aunt Nora.

*Hair like moonlight*...

Oh, God, she thought, as memory stabbed at her suddenly, viciously. Not dead as she'd believed and hoped, but brutally alive.

She sat rigidly, her nails digging into the palms of her hands as she tried to force that particular memory back into the oblivion it deserved.

No one would ever say it to her again. She'd made sure of that long ago, leaving the long silky strands on the floor at the hairdressing salon in Haylesford in exchange for a *gamine* crop with feathery tendrils framing her face and giving emphasis to her high cheekbones.

Yet another difference between us, she thought, as she made herself think about Millie again.

She looks like Mum, and I take after Dad's side of the family, she reflected, swallowing past the lump in her throat. He always claimed he had Viking ancestry and that's where our colouring came from. On the other hand, he tended to wing his way through life like Millie, while my mother was the steady, sober member of the partnership. As I believed I was.

But whatever the reason for Aunt Nora's reluctance to take them on, it couldn't be a dislike of children because she ran a private junior school for girls and a very successful one, catering for those needing extra help to pass the examinations for their very expensive senior schools, or, as it was known, a crammer.

Not that she and Millie were ever enrolled at Meade House School, even though they were both under thirteen. Instead, they were both placed very firmly in the state system.

Her long-term plans for them, however, she'd kept to herself, Selena thought drily.

She drank some more coffee, wondering why she was re-treading these well-worn paths all over again. Especially when she'd told herself the best way to survive was to shut the door on the past. Think only of the future.

Or was this simply deliberate prevarication? Delaying the moment when she'd have to deal with Millie's letter, still in the kitchen, silently demanding her unwilling attention.

Time to get it over with, she decided as she finished her coffee and went indoors.

The single piece of paper inside the envelope looked as if it had been ripped from a small notebook.

'Lena' Millie had written. 'We have to talk. It's an emergency, so please, please call me.' She'd added the telephone number, including the code, and signed off 'M'.

Short, but not too sweet, thought Selena. And it's almost certainly about money because Rhymnos is bound to be having its share of economic problems.

Or has her life on a small Greek island already palled and could this cry for help involve a one-way ticket back to Britain?

But to do what—and to live where? Well, hardly here, that was for sure, sharing a cramped bedroom with a three-quarter-sized bed, not to mention a shower room not much bigger than a cupboard.

And apart from some undistinguished GCSEs, Millie had no qualifications for any career except bar work or waitressing. And she'd probably had her fill of both by now.

Surely she can't imagine there's a remote possibility that Aunt Nora's been in touch and all is forgiven?

If so, dream on, Millie, she thought. She's out of our lives for good and all.

And why didn't you ring me if it's all so urgent? Especially as I sent you my number along with the address.

She realised she'd crumpled the letter in her hand, and smoothed it out again on the work surface.

The phone number Millie had given clearly demonstrated that she was still living with Kostas at his *taverna*, named Amelia in her honour. But maybe that was only temporary.

And although it was tempting to take the coward's way out and pretend the letter had never come, Millie was, in spite of everything, her sister and wanted her help.

She said aloud, 'I can't let her down.'

Steeling herself, she picked up the phone. It was answered on the second ring. A man's voice.

She kept her voice cool and steady. 'Kostas? It's Selena.'

'Ah, sister, you have called.' Across the miles, she could hear the relief in his tone. 'How good to hear you. But I knew it would be so. I told my Amelia that she must not disturb herself with worry.'

'Things have obviously been—difficult for you all,' she said. *And that's putting it mildly.*

*'Po, po, po.* Now we look for better times.'

'Yes,' she said. 'Of course.' She paused. 'Is Millie around? Can I speak to her?'

'At this moment, no, sister. The doctor has ordered she must rest, and she is sleeping.'

'The doctor,' Selena repeated, frowning. 'You mean she's ill? What's wrong with her? Is it serious?'

'I cannot say. It is a woman's thing, and she feels

scared and very much alone.' He hesitated. 'My mother is here, of course, but—it is not easy, you understand.'

I bet, thought Selena, remembering Anna Papoulis in her unrelieved widow's mourning, her headscarf framing her sharp face with its narrow-lipped, bitter mouth set in resentment of her son's foreign bride.

However, it seemed as if the marriage was surviving, which was some relief.

'It is you that she wants. Again and again she says it, and she weeps.' His tone became eager. 'If you would come here—be with her for a while—she would soon be better. I know it. And there is a room for you here with us. I prepared it in hope.'

She was shocked into silence. And disbelief.

Rhymnos, she thought. He actually thinks I can go back to Rhymnos? After everything that happened? He must be crazy.

'No,' she said at last, her voice harsh. 'That's impossible. You know it is. I—I'm needed here.'

'But things are different now,' he persisted. 'You have nothing to fear, sister. People have gone,' he added, his voice heavy with meaning. 'The island has changed. You will be safe here. Safe with us.'

*I thought I was safe before. Believed Millie was the one in danger. Yet I was the one to be betrayed and I still have the scars.*

He went on quickly, 'And my Amelia wants so badly to see you—to be with you. I cannot bear for her to be disappointed.'

No, she thought. That's how it all began. Because Millie mustn't be disappointed. Because two of her classmates were having a holiday in Greece, for the first time without their parents, and asked her to go with them. And she cried when Aunt Nora said, 'At seventeen? Absolutely not.'

Tears on their own probably wouldn't have worked, but reinforcements arrived in the shape of Mrs Raymond, mother of Daisy, whose idea the trip had been, and, in her way, as formidable as Aunt Nora.

'I think one has to allow them some independence at their age,' she'd pronounced majestically. 'Demonstrate that we trust them. After all, they'll all be off to university next year.'

Daisy and Fiona, perhaps, Selena had thought drily. Millie—only if she started doing some work.

'And Rhymnos is only small and quiet, not crowded with nightclubs, which means fewer opportunities for mischief,' Mrs Raymond had added. 'The hotel, too, is family run and has a good reputation. The girls are so keen for Millie to go with them, and she's bound to be disappointed if she's left behind. Besides, there's safety in numbers, you know.'

It all sounded too good to be true, Selena had thought with sudden unease, hoping that Aunt Nora would stick to her guns.

But, albeit reluctantly, she'd eventually agreed, leaving Selena to shrug and decide it was none of her business.

Which only proved how wrong it was possible to be.

Because, suddenly and incredibly, it had become her business, turning her entire life upside down.

Kostas was speaking again. 'If it is a matter of cost, I

shall happily pay the airfare to Mykonos, and the ferry transfer. I ask only that you come to us—for Amelia's sake. She hopes so much to see you.'

She said crisply, 'That was hardly the impression she gave when we last spoke.'

He sighed. 'But in all families, sister, things are said in anger and then regretted. And I am relying on your compassion for a sick girl.'

Selena bit her lip. Put like that, she thought, she could hardly refuse. And yet she was aware again of that odd sense of unease. Although, he'd said things had changed...

But I haven't changed, she thought. I know that now. And perhaps I never will until I have the courage to face my demons and put them finally to rest. And maybe that time has come.

She took a deep, painful breath. 'Very well, Kostas, I'll come as soon as I can get a flight—which I will pay for myself, thanks all the same. I'll be in touch when I have the details.' She added, 'And wish Millie well for me.'

She occupied the rest of her day with some heavy duty housework, trying to ignore the small voice in her head telling her that she'd clearly learned nothing from her past mistakes and was, once again, behaving like an idiot.

Because she knew how doubtful it was that Millie would make the same concessions for her, if their positions were reversed.

But she could probably live with herself, she thought

drily. Whereas I couldn't—especially if this illness of hers turns out to be something really serious.

And, in that case, what kind of medical attention could Millie expect in so small a place?

If she needs to come back to England with me, I'll deal with it, even if it means finding an even bigger place.

She decided to have an early night, in view of all she had to do the following day, hoping, too, that sleep would silence that little warning voice—at least for a while.

As she undressed, she embarked on a mental list of what she'd need to take with her to Rhymnos, remembering that the high summer temperature could soar to forty degrees plus.

Reaching for her nightdress, she glimpsed herself in the wall mirror and paused, wondering if the events of the past year had altered her in any significant way. But, apart from her severely shorn hair, her critical gaze could see no real change. Her breasts were still high and rounded, her waist small, her stomach flat and her hips gently curved.

I look, she told herself ironically, almost untouched. And found her laugh turning into a sob.

She spent a wretched, restless night and was sorely tempted, when her radio alarm went into action, simply to silence it, pull the covers over her head and stay where she was.

The coward's way out, she thought wryly as she swung her feet to the floor and headed to the shower.

Her first visit was to the letting agency, to register her new requirements, followed by a wander round a cheap and cheerful fashion store which still had a few pairs of cotton cut-off pants, tee shirts and even a one-piece swimsuit available in her size and within her limited budget.

Working on the premise that she wasn't sure how long her stay would last or if she'd be returning alone, she booked a single flight at the travel agency, and bought some euros, knowing she would have to use them carefully because she could afford no more.

But her most difficult task was still ahead of her, she reminded herself as she emerged into the street, subjecting her, no doubt, to more disapproval and more pressure. Except this time, she'd have a positive response to make. An actual workable plan for the future.

She heard her name called and turning saw Janet Forbes coming towards her smiling.

'I'm glad I've seen you,' she said. 'I was planning to get in touch anyway and have a chat, over an iced coffee maybe, or are you too busy?'

'No, that would be great.'

They went to a cafe with a veranda overlooking the river, its banks busy with families sunbathing, eating ice cream and feeding the ducks.

'I wanted to say how delighted I am that we'll be working together again next year,' Mrs Forbes began as they sipped their coffees under the shade of the awning.

'Megan was a nice girl and very conscientious, but I always felt that she was simply filling in time. Whereas you…'

She paused. 'I wondered if you'd ever considered getting a BEd and becoming a teacher yourself, because I'd say you were a natural.' She added swiftly, 'Not that I want to lose you, of course. Please don't think that.'

Selena was all set to declare herself perfectly happy with her lot. Instead, to her own astonishment, she heard herself say, 'I did start training but got no further than the second year.' She forced a smile. 'Family problems.'

'Well, that's a great shame.' Mrs Forbes gave her a thoughtful look. 'You could always go back to it, you know. It's never too late to start again.'

That, Selena thought, is what I keep telling myself. Maybe it's time I believed it.

'One day, perhaps,' she said. 'I mean, I'd love to, but right now I have—other priorities.'

'Well, do bear it in mind for the future.' Mrs Forbes got to her feet, collecting her bags. 'I hate to see talent wasted.' She patted Selena on the shoulder. 'Maybe when your family problems are behind you.'

Except, thought Selena, watching her go, you don't know the half of them. And I can never tell you, or anyone else, what happened two years ago.

Or that I'm still struggling with the aftermath.

# CHAPTER TWO

SHE SUPPOSED SHE ought to move. Go back to the store and buy some of the clothes she'd seen. The absolute minimum would do and was all she could afford anyway.

But being accustomed to living on not much could stand her in good stead if her life changed in the way she hoped.

Not 'if', she told herself, but 'when'.

And in celebration, she recklessly ordered another iced coffee.

How strange, she thought, when she'd been watching Janet Forbes so closely, admiring her classroom technique, her patience and ability to engage the children, and keep them interested and focussed, that, all the time, Mrs Forbes had been watching her. Deciding to encourage her into teaching.

Not blackmail her into it.

She'd been sixteen, quietly delighted with her GCSE results when Aunt Nora had dropped her bombshell. Informed her that all her university expenses would be paid as long as she, and eventually Millie, too, agreed to teach at Meade House after graduation.

Otherwise, Selena could forget the Sixth Form and college, leave her comprehensive school and find a job.

'I had to settle your late parents' debts as well as bearing the costs of your upbringing,' her aunt had stated coldly. 'I expect to be repaid, Selena. And Amelia, of course, will have to do the same.'

She paused, allowing that to sink in. 'And kindly stop looking as if your death sentence had just been pronounced. At Meade House, you and your sister will be guaranteed a continuing home, careers and security. A little gratitude would not come amiss.'

How am I supposed to look, Selena had wondered, when every plan—every dream I had of getting away from Haylesford and being my own person—has been virtually knocked on the head?

For a moment, she'd been prepared to say *To hell with it* and take the risk, but she knew that she could not make choices that would also affect the future of fourteen-year-old Millie. That was neither right nor fair.

And once her agreement had been obtained, however unwilling, there had been a perceptible easing of Aunt Nora's strict regime, leading eventually, inevitably to Millie being permitted her Greek holiday with her friends.

Selena had found a vacation job in a cafe, one which turned out to be short-lived because one showery July day her aunt slipped and fell in her garden and ended up in hospital with a broken leg.

Aunt Nora, ensconced in a comfortable private room, received her sourly. 'They won't allow me to go home until I've mastered using these crutches.' She gestured disdainfully to where they stood, propped against the wall. 'But even with them, I'm going to require help, and Amelia, of course, is leaving for Greece in ten days' time.'

Lucky Millie, Selena thought grimly.

As she'd suspected 'patient' was hardly the word to describe her aunt, who kept her on the run from first thing in the morning until last thing at night, with the help of the little handbell she kept beside her at all times.

In addition, Millie had fussed endlessly over her packing, claiming exclusive access to the washing machine and ironing board, and providing Aunt Nora with another excuse to grumble.

It was almost a relief when Mrs Raymond arrived with Daisy and Fiona to drive them all to the airport.

One less problem to handle, Selena thought, as she closed the front door.

'Dr Bishop says I shall need physiotherapy when the plaster is eventually removed,' her aunt announced the following week. 'He has given me a list of reliable practitioners who pay private visits.'

'Isn't it available on the National Health Service?' asked Selena.

'Not to the extent that I shall require,' Aunt Nora said coldly. 'Dr Bishop says it was such a serious fracture that I shall probably have to learn to walk all over again.'

Selena thought drily that Dr Bishop, rightly nicknamed Old Smoothie by Millie, excelled at telling her aunt exactly what she wanted to hear, and hoped the physio would have more sense.

And, talking of Millie, apart from an initial text announcing that Rhymnos was great, they'd heard nothing from her.

Still, she decided, philosophically, the parents of Daisy and Fiona were probably in the same boat, and, anyway, wasn't no news supposed to be good news?

She'd been into town the afternoon the girls were due back, taking a list of her aunt's requests to the public library. She expected Millie to have arrived when she got back, yet there was no clutter of luggage in the hall.

The flight must have been delayed, she thought, then heard her aunt calling her, her voice high and angry, and found her sitting upright, two bright spots of colour in her cheeks emphasising her unusual pallor.

She checked, the terrible memory of her parents' accident striking at her, making her feel sick to her stomach with fright. 'Has—has something happened?'

'Oh, yes.' Her aunt's voice shook with fury. 'Your sister, it seems, has involved herself with some local yob on that island and decided to stay there—to set up house with him. Apparently she'd gone from her hotel room this morning with all her things. The other girls had to leave without her.

'Well, I won't have it. I will not allow her to disgrace me, to make me ridiculous in front of the whole town— a child of her age. However there's nothing I can do about it, so you'll have to go over there and bring her back.' She added ominously, 'Before too much harm is done.'

Selena sank down on the nearest chair. Typical, she thought bitterly, that her aunt should see the situation in terms of personal disgrace rather than the danger to Millie and the potential ruin of her future.

She said, 'Who is the man? Do Daisy and Fiona know?'

'It seems he's the barman at the Hotel Olympia where they were staying. His name is Kostas.' Aunt Nora pronounced the name with acute distaste then held out a piece of paper that had been crumpled in her hand. 'She left this note.' She shuddered. 'Mrs Raymond could hardly look me in the eye. I blame her entirely for allowing this trip in the first place and then badgering me to let Amelia be part of it.

'But that, of course, won't stop her telling the entire town what's happened. She's probably already started.'

Selena read the note frowningly. Millie said simply that she was not coming back to England because she loved Kostas and was staying with him.

So, not much room for negotiation there, she thought.

'As you can see, there's no time to lose.' Aunt Nora was regaining some of her old briskness. 'So, you go there, you find her and you bring her back. That's all there is to be said.'

She added decisively, 'I will not have my plans for the future of the school wrecked by some childish infatuation. Men like this barman should be locked up.'

Selena tried to reason with her, pointing out that Millie was not a child and it might be better to let her realise her mistake and return of her own accord.

And how, she asked, would her aunt manage without her, only to discover that Aunt Nora had already booked a live-in carer.

'Terribly expensive,' she'd said sourly. 'I hope Amelia realises the inconvenience she's causing.'

But nothing Selena said made the slightest difference, which was why, only two days later she found herself on board the ferry from Mykonos with the harbour at Rhymnos already in sight.

She was in no mood to appreciate the attractive scene it presented, with its tangle of *caiques* and motor cruisers, and beyond them the row of *tavernas* and shops fronting the waterside.

And above them, on the hillside and not nearly as impressive as its name, picked out in large blue letters on the white walls, stood the Hotel Olympia.

Enemy in sight, thought Selena grimly as she picked up the big canvas satchel that served as her luggage and slung it over her shoulder.

As she came ashore she was assailed by a chorus of whistles and other bids to attract her attention by the young men mending fishing nets or waiting on tables at the *tavernas*.

No wonder Millie, released from the kind of purdah existing at Meade House Cottage, had been such easy game for an unscrupulous local, she thought.

Daisy and Fiona, with obvious reluctance, had volunteered a few details—his full name, Kostas Papoulis, young, good-looking, full of himself, and—with a shrug—sexy.

Besides, Daisy had added with faint malice, she hadn't thought that he was that interested in Millie. Just—playing around.

Selena wanted to slap her. Hard.

On the other hand, if this had also occurred to Millie by now, it might make her own task much easier.

The short walk up to the hotel was blisteringly hot, and she began to think longingly of iced water.

From the road, a path led up through borders bright with flowers to a terrace running the length of the frontage, and a pair of glass doors.

The foyer was light and airy, with a marble floor and a polished reception desk, currently unattended.

But Selena headed straight for the door labelled 'Bar', immediately opposite, and, drawing a deep breath, she walked in.

Once again, it seemed entirely deserted. Where was everyone? she wondered, as she looked about her. It was as if the entire establishment had been abducted by aliens.

Which the aliens could have done with her good wishes, she thought, just as long as they hadn't taken Millie.

But as she hesitated, she heard above the hiss and bubble of the coffee machine on the end of the counter, an unmistakable chink of bottles coming from behind a curtained doorway at the rear of the bar itself.

She walked to the counter, sliding her bag from her shoulder to the floor, and coughed loudly. When there was no immediate response, she followed it up with an imperative, 'Hello.'

The curtain was swept back, and a man appeared, clipboard in hand, his frowning gaze scanning her impatiently.

Selena found she was staring back, hoping she didn't

look as shocked as she felt because he bore little resemblance to the arrogant young stud described by Daisy, or any of the grinning lads she'd encountered at the harbour.

For one thing he was clearly older, probably in his late twenties, tall, swarthy, and in need of both a haircut and a shave, with a lean muscular body clad in jeans and a faded red polo shirt that emphasised the easy strength of his chest and shoulders.

Not conventionally handsome, she thought, aware her throat had suddenly tightened, his dark eyes brilliant, the nose and chin strongly marked, the mouth cool and sculpted with a firmness that suggested he was very much in charge of himself and his surroundings. Someone with—presence. And more.

She thought, *Oh, God, Millie, you stupid, stupid girl. He's miles out of your league. What have you done?*

He broke the silence, his voice deep and resonant as he addressed her in what was apparently German.

She said, 'I don't understand,' and saw his scrutiny sharpen and become more searching.

If you're thinking I could be trouble, you've got it in one, she informed him silently.

His English was excellent, with only a faint trace of an accent. 'I apologise for my mistake, *thespinis*. I was misled by your hair.' His gaze rested on the gleaming pale blonde mass tumbling over her shoulders, and for a startling moment, it was as if he'd touched it. Run his fingers through the length of it.

'But I was telling you that the bar is closed at this time of day, unless, of course, you wish for coffee.'

She lifted her chin. 'No thank you. I've only come for my sister.'

'Then I am afraid you must look elsewhere.' He glanced pointedly past her at the unoccupied array of glass-topped tables and small easy chairs, set in comfortable groups. 'Most of our guests are by the pool at the back of the hotel, or on the beach. Is she a resident?'

'You tell me. After all you're the only one likely to know her exact whereabouts.' She glanced at her watch.

'So shall we stop playing games? Just take me to her and she'll be off your hands and on the way back to Mykonos and the airport on the next ferry.'

'An excellent plan.' His voice was crisper. 'But there is a problem. I do not know either your sister's identity or where she may be found. Except it is plainly not here.'

Selena gasped. 'You mean she's already left? She's on her way home?' She glared at him. 'I suppose I should be grateful to you, but I'm finding it difficult.'

'It is also unnecessary. I was not aware of her presence here, or her departure. I suggest you conduct your enquiries elsewhere,' he added with cold finality and turned as if to go back to the store room.

'And I suggest you answer my questions,' she flung after him, aware that she was trembling inside, and not simply with temper at being so summarily dismissed. 'Otherwise I shall go to the police and tell them you've taken advantage of a vulnerable seventeen-year-old. That you've kept her here to have sex with her, forcing her friends to return to the UK without her, and causing endless worry to her family.'

She added contemptuously, 'I thought the Greeks were supposed to respect foreign travellers.'

'We do,' he said. 'Although your female compatriots do not always make it easy.' The contempt was echoed and the frown was back in force. 'She was staying here, your sister and her friends? Their names?'

'Raymond, Marsden and—and Blake.' She heard her voice quiver slightly and snatched at her self-command.

'Ah, yes.' He nodded. 'I remember some of the staff speaking of them.' His tone suggested the comments were not to their credit.

Well, he was the last person with any right to pass judgement.

'Whatever their opinions, nothing justifies your be-haviour, Mr Papoulis.' She was about to say 'And I in-sist you bring Millie here immediately,' when she was stopped in her tracks by the realisation that he'd started to laugh.

'I'm glad you're amused,' she said scornfully. 'How-ever, the police may not share your sense of humour.'

'They may,' he said, still grinning. 'When they hear I have been mistaken for my own barman. And they would undoubtedly tell you that, when you burst in, all guns blazing, *thespinis*, you should make sure they are aimed at the right target.'

He put down the clipboard and held out his hand. 'Allow me to introduce myself. I am Alexis Constan-tinou and I own this hotel. Kostas is merely employed here, when he can take the trouble to work,' he added sardonically. 'But at least I know the reason for his absence this time, and that he cannot use the excuse that he is ill.'

Numb with embarrassment, and bitterly aware of the mockery in his dark eyes, Selena allowed her fingers to be gripped briefly in his.

'So Kostas has sweet-talked your young sister into his bed,' he went on musingly. 'Strange. He usually confines his attentions to rather older women—the single, the divorced, so...' He paused, his gaze once more drifting down her hair. 'So—she must have made quite an impression.'

Her skin warming, she said tautly, 'I don't find that particularly reassuring.'

'Nor would I,' he said unexpectedly, 'if she was my sister.'

He turned to the shelf of bottles behind him. 'I think you need a drink, *thespinis*, and so do I.' He poured something amber into two glasses and gave her one. 'Five-star Metaxa,' he said. 'A universal remedy. Especially for shock.'

She said tautly, 'You don't seem particularly shocked over your employee's behaviour.'

'No,' he agreed. 'However, it is an irritation.'

He came round the bar and took the drinks to a table, motioning her to join him. She obeyed reluctantly, bringing her satchel with her.

Alexis Constantinou eyed it with faint amusement. 'You travel light, Kyria Blake.'

'It's going to be a brief visit, Mr Constantinou. I intend to find my sister and persuade her to leave this—

this cut-price Casanova she's involved with and come home.'

His amusement deepened. 'You have quite a turn of phrase, *thespinis*.'

'Thank you.' She added tautly, 'And if I may say so, perhaps you ought to exercise more vigilance over your staff's out-of-hours activities.'

'I make sure they do their job,' he said. 'I do not claim to be anyone's moral guardian. And perhaps your sister and her friends are the ones in need of guidance.'

'How dare you,' she flared. 'Millie is totally inexperienced. He's taken advantage of her innocence.'

'You paint a moving picture,' he said, clearly remaining unmoved. 'Now let us drink.' He raised his glass, touching it to the one she was holding, '*Yamas*. That means—to our health.'

She didn't like the way the toast seemed to unite them, but took a cautious sip, suppressing a gasp as it trailed fire down her throat.

'What is that?' she asked when she could speak.

'Brandy. To give you strength for your search. And—to calm you.'

She bit her lip. 'I'm perfectly calm, thank you.' And wished it was true. Because she was suddenly all too aware of him watching her. Glanced away and found herself instead looking at the hand clasping his glass. At the long fingers and well-kept nails, and the way his thumb was playing with the glass's stem.

Even with the width of the table between them, he seemed too close for comfort.

She went on hurriedly, 'If you'll just give me Mr

Papoulis's address, I'll go and let you get back to—
whatever you were doing.'

'Stock-taking,' he said. 'As for Kostas's address,' he
added with a shrug, 'I doubt if that will help. Like the
rest of the staff, when he is working, he has a room here,
but this, I am told, he has not used for several days.'

The implication in his words was obvious, Selena
thought, swallowing.

'And when he's not working?' she demanded.

'He lives with his widowed mother,' he said. 'But
she is very pious, so I doubt you will find your Millie
there, either.'

She said half to herself, 'Then what am I going to
do?'

'I am sure that is not a request for my advice,' he
drawled. 'But I shall offer it just the same. Go home,
*thespinis*, and wait for your sister to come to her senses.'

She took another gulp of brandy. 'And if he's keeping her here against her will?'

'Once again you are allowing your taste for the dramatic to run away with you,' Alexis Constantinou said
softly. 'Kostas, believe me, has no need to use force.'

'You take all this so lightly.' Her voice shook. 'When
I'm worried sick, and I—I can't leave without her.'

She paused. 'I shall have to go to the police.'

'I would prefer that not to happen.'

Her voice rose indignantly. 'You're actually protecting him?'

'No,' he said, with faint grimness. 'I am protecting
the reputation of my hotel. And for that, I am prepared to
help you. Give me a day, maybe two, to make enquiries.

To find where he is and if your sister is indeed with him. But that is all. After that, it is up to you. Do you agree?'

Selena stared down at the table. Almost in spite of herself, she could feel the warmth of the brandy quelling her inner trembling. A sense of something like hope growing in its place. Which was, of course, quite ridiculous under the circumstances.

She said, 'How do I know I can trust you?'

'Because stock-taking bores me,' he said. 'I want my barman back. His absence is inconvenient.'

She glared at him. She said mutinously, 'In that case—I suppose we have a deal.' She reached for her satchel and got to her feet. 'Thank you for the drink, and I hope your plan succeeds.'

'Wait,' he said. 'I need to know where to contact you.' He eyed her narrowly. 'You have made a reservation, found a place to stay, of course.'

She hesitated. Fatally. 'Not yet, but I'm sure I'll find somewhere.'

'I do not doubt it.' His tone was cynical. 'With that hair and those eyes, *pedhi mou*, you will be overwhelmed with offers in the first moment. In fact, your sister, wherever she may be, is probably much safer.'

She was shaken by that altogether too intimate reference to her appearance. She said coldly, 'I'm a university student, Mr Constantinou. I can look after myself. I can make my own arrangements—and my own enquiries.'

'The English, I think, have a saying,' he drawled. '"Famous last words." Perhaps you know it.'

'Nevertheless…'

'Nevertheless, *thespinis*, you will not go into the

town asking for a room to rent. I shall not permit it. Besides, how can you enquire about anything when you do not speak Greek?'

He rose to his feet. 'The Olympia is fully booked, but I have a small flat on the top floor for my personal use. You may stay there.'

'We have another quaint old saying in my country.' She faced him, lifting her chin. '"Out of the frying pan into the fire." Maybe you've heard that, too.'

He said silkily, 'And you, *pedhi mou*, should not jump to conclusions. I shall stay at my house, the Villa Helios, on the other side of the island. A safe enough distance, wouldn't you say?'

There were a lot of things she would like to have said, but she only managed a reluctant, 'Thank you.'

Alexis Constantinou nodded. 'Now I will speak to my housekeeper about your accommodation. And you perhaps should finish your brandy.'

As he walked to the door, Selena said, 'Why have you changed your mind suddenly? I—I don't understand.'

'You think I should not concern myself over the wellbeing of an innocent and inexperienced girl?'

'A moment ago you were implying that Millie's problems are all of her own making.'

'I still do,' he said. 'But the innocent I speak of is not your sister, *thespinis*, but yourself.'

And he walked out of the bar, leaving Selena staring after him.

# CHAPTER THREE

'EXCUSE ME, DO you want to order anything else? Only there are people waiting for tables.'

The aggrieved tone of the waitress jolted Selena back to the present.

'I've finished, thank you.' She tried a smile. 'I'm sorry, I was miles away.'

Worlds away. An ocean of pain away, she thought as the girl gathered up the used crockery and walked away with a faint sniff.

Back in the honeyed trap that she'd thought was kindness. Caught by a man who was neither innocent nor inexperienced.

And now she had to go back to where it all happened. To Rhymnos—the place where she'd ruined her life and broken her heart.

At the same time, it was her chance to prove to herself that she had survived. Even mended.

As she left, she passed the young couple waiting for her table, and saw that the man was wearing a baby sling across his chest, cradling an infant obviously in its first weeks of life, its over-large cotton sun hat slipping down over a red, crumpled, sleeping face.

Saw, too, the way the young father looked down proudly at his child, then exchanged smiles with the pretty girl beside him in shared delight.

Selena felt a sudden twist of agony inside her, as if a hand had reached into her and wrenched at her heart, then she turned slowly and walked away, to tackle her final and most important problem.

The interview had proved just as difficult as she'd anticipated, she thought unhappily as she walked home.

'You're going on holiday?' Mrs Talbot had radiated disapproval. 'Do you think that's appropriate?'

'Unavoidable, I'm afraid,' Selena had returned quietly. 'And it's hardly a holiday. My sister is ill.'

'All the same, you'll be missing scheduled visits, which is very disappointing—for everyone.'

She was almost tempted to cancel, but, in the end, she simply sent Kostas a text with the time of her flight.

She made herself a cheese salad before she emptied and cleaned the fridge. Then she stuffed the contents of her linen basket into a large carrier bag, and set off to the nearby launderette.

She'd taken a book to read, but she found it difficult to lose herself in the story when other thoughts, other memories persisted in intervening. In pushing aside all other considerations.

Forcing her to go back to that first day on Rhymnos and that fateful encounter at the Hotel Olympia.

Left alone in the bar, she'd taken one more sip of brandy, then pushed the glass away. She'd already made one idiotic mistake, she reminded herself, and there was no need to muddle her thinking any further.

Because she had to decide very quickly whether to remain here and accept the help Alexis Constantinou had offered, or grab her bag and run.

In principle, her mission had seemed simple enough. Come to the hotel, confront this Kostas, who might be having second thoughts himself by now, and convince Millie that a holiday romance was not a commitment for life, and it was time to go home.

It had never occurred to her, or presumably Aunt Nora, that the pair might disappear.

And where would she go, anyway? If the Olympia was full, it might not be easy to find a respectable alternative—although Alexis Constantinou's offer of his private flat hardly qualified as that, either, in spite of his assurances.

And relying solely on a Greek phrasebook wasn't going to be much help in tracking down the runaways.

I should have done more homework in advance, she thought bitterly. If I'd been allowed to, of course.

However, she was here now, and her main concern was finding Millie, for which, galling as it might be, she probably needed the help of Alexis Constantinou.

It doesn't matter, she told herself, gritting her teeth. After all, the sooner you trace Millie, the quicker you can leave.

Suddenly restless, she rose and wandered over to the glass doors, which ran the length of one side of the bar, and walked out on to the balcony beyond with its flight of marble steps leading down to another area of garden, bright with flowers and shrubs and surrounded by hibiscus hedges. And beyond that, hazy with heat, the infinite blue of the Aegean.

Apart from a faint sound of splashing from the pool area, it was very quiet.

If I was here for a different reason, just one guest among many, I'd probably not want to leave, either, she realised with a swift pang.

She remained where she was, letting the peace soak into her, until a sound from the bar behind her made her turn hurriedly in time to see a tall, thin man with a heavy black moustache place a tray with a pot of coffee and a plate of pastries on her table.

'For you, *thespinis*,' he announced. 'Kyrios Alexis, he say it is long before dinner.'

'Oh,' Selena said disconcerted. 'Thank you.' Then remembering one of the words she'd learned on the plane, she added, *'Efharisto.'*

He inclined his head. *'Parakalo,'* he returned politely. 'I am Stelios and I manage the hotel for Kyrios Alexis. Anything you wish for, please ask me.'

Presumably that did not include a missing sister, Selena thought as he vanished.

The coffee was a strong filter brew, and the food turned out to be delicious little cheese tarts, still warm from the oven. Selena ate every scrap.

She had just drained her final cup when she was joined by a middle-aged woman wearing a neat black dress and an air of unmistakable authority.

She pointed to herself. 'Androula, *thespinis*. Housekeeper. Your room waits for you.'

She picked up the satchel and waited for Selena to accompany her.

A lift at the side of the foyer whisked them to the third floor. Androula led the way along the corridor to a pair of double doors at the end, which she unlocked, then stood aside allowing Selena to precede her into a spacious sitting room, with comfortable sofas and chairs upholstered in deep blue linen grouped round a massive square coffee table, its surface tiled in cream and gold.

As she looked round her, two girls emerged from another room, one carrying an expensive leather suitcase, the other a linen laundry bag.

As they passed Selena, they smiled shyly, but their eyes were alive with curiosity.

They must be wondering why they've been asked to clear the decks, she thought drily. However, it seemed that their boss was a man of his word after all and she only wished she could feel more at ease with the situation.

The bedroom was uncompromisingly masculine, almost disturbingly so, with shutters at the windows instead of drapes, dark fitted furniture, and what seemed to Selena to be an ultra-wide bed, made up with immaculate white linen, and a brown and gold coverlet in a Greek key pattern folded at its foot.

A door in the corner led into a bathroom almost as big as the bedroom, with a large walk-in shower as well as a tub, and twin basins in the long mirrored vanity unit, indicating, perhaps, that the owner did not always lack for company.

As if, she reminded herself swiftly, it was any business of hers.

Nevertheless it seemed she would be maintained pretty much in the lap of luxury during her brief stay, although she would have to make it clear to Mr Constantinou at their next encounter that she'd come prepared to pay for her board and lodging.

At least Aunt Nora has allowed for that, she thought. So I won't be obliged to be in his debt more than I can help.

She turned to Androula. 'Thank you.' She made an awkward gesture. 'It's lovely.'

The housekeeper inclined her head politely. 'You rest now,' she said. 'I will send someone to bring you to dinner at eight o clock.'

And on that, she departed, closing the outer door behind her. And, Selena realised in horror, locking it, too.

She was just about to rush over and beat on the panels, shouting 'Come back,' when she saw, just in time, another key lying in the centre of the coffee table, and realised her host was probably not the floor's sole occupant. And allowed herself a faint groan of relief that she hadn't made an utter fool of herself twice in one hour.

She's right, she thought. Maybe I do need to rest. Also—get a grip.

She retrieved her forlorn cotton robe from her bag and went to the bathroom, where she took a long, satisfying soak in the tub, then stretched out in the middle of that vast bed and gratefully closed her eyes. She was asleep within minutes.

It was already after seven when she awoke, and for

a while she lay watching with languid pleasure how the evening sunlight slatted through the shutters across the marble tiles.

Yes, she had to get ready, but it wouldn't take long. There weren't any anxious choices to make over how to dress for dinner. There was her denim skirt with a white top, or her denim skirt and the other white top.

Travelling light has its advantages, Mr Constantinou, she addressed him silently as she wriggled off the bed.

It was the prettier of the two maids she'd seen earlier who came to collect her and escort her to the restaurant on the ground floor, and her sideways glance, although polite, conveyed she was not greatly impressed by either the denim skirt or the other white top, or by the fact that Selena, on some inexplicable impulse, had plaited her hair into the severe braid preferred by Aunt Nora.

But then, thought Selena, I'm here on business, not out to impress—anyone.

The dining room was a large, airy room, most of its tables already occupied, and Selena attracted little attention as a waiter conducted her to a secluded corner partly screened from the rest of the room by a trellis supporting foliage plants growing in terracotta pots.

As she sat down, Selena realised it was the first time she'd ever eaten alone in a hotel. What a sheltered life you've led, Miss Blake, she mocked herself.

It had only just dawned on her that the table was set for two when Alexis Constantinou appeared, saunter-ing across the dining room, exchanging smiling greet-

ings with the other diners as he approached, and clearly
heading straight for her corner.

*Oh, please no*, she begged under her breath as her
tense fingers crumpled the linen napkin she was spreading on her lap.

'*Kalispera*,' he said as he took the chair opposite.
'That means good evening.'

'Yes,' she said shortly. 'I picked up a few words on
the flight. That was one of them.'

No one would have mistaken him for a barman now,
even someone with an Olympic gold for leaping to conclusions, she conceded ruefully.

He'd shaved, for one thing, and the elegant, pale grey
suit he was wearing was offset by a charcoal shirt, carrying the unmistakable sheen of silk, and open at the
neck, revealing several inches of bronzed, hair-darkened
skin, which it would be safer to ignore.

No, not handsome, she thought in sudden bewilderment, but stunningly, mind-blowingly attractive in a
way she'd never encountered before. Or never been
aware of, at any rate.

By contrast, she must look like something the cat
dragged in.

'Excellent.' He smiled at her. 'Perhaps during our acquaintance, we will be able to extend your repertoire.'

'I doubt if there'll be time.' She adjusted a perfectly
placed fork, crossly aware that her skin was warming.
She added hurriedly, 'I'm hoping that you have some
news for me.'

'I have certainly made enquiries among the staff,'
he returned. 'But so far, without result.'

'Perhaps they're shielding him.'

'I never thought he was that popular,' he said drily. He paused. 'It seems, this time, he took the trouble to be discreet.'

*This time*, Selena repeated under her breath and winced.

He saw and said more gently, 'Forgive me. I meant it might indicate that this time he could be genuinely in love.'

'In two weeks?' Her objection was instant and vehement. 'That's ridiculous. No one could possibly fall truly in love that quickly.'

'You don't think so?'

'Of course not. People have to—to like each other first. Be friends. Enjoy each other's company. Have shared interests, and learn respect for each other's opinions.' My God, she thought. I sound like my great-grandmother.

His brows lifted. 'That is how it was for you?' His tone was politely interested.

And what was she supposed to say to that? To admit she could count the number of her dates, all strictly casual, on the fingers of one hand?

It might be best, safer, she thought uneasily, to make him think she was involved. 'Yes,' she said defiantly. 'As a matter of fact.'

'And that is how it sounds, *pedhi mou*.' His dark eyes glinted at her. 'Matter of fact.'

A change of subject seemed well overdue. She said, 'What do you keep calling me?' She tried to pronounce the words as he had.

'It means—my little one.'

She lifted her chin. 'Then please don't say it again. It's—demeaning. I am not a child.'

*'Po, po, po,'* he said softly. 'Then why tie back your beautiful hair like a little girl at school?'

'Because it's cool,' she said. 'And neat.'

'Ah,' he said. 'That is how you see yourself, perhaps?'

'I'm too busy to give it much thought,' she retorted. 'Besides, all that's important to me right now is my sister's well-being.' She paused. 'How do we go about finding her?'

'Quietly,' he said. 'Another reason not to go to the police. People talk and news travels fast. It is better your sister does not know you are here to collect her, so she and Kostas do not run away to another island, or even to the mainland and add to your difficulties.'

He beckoned and a waiter arrived at the table with an ice bucket, a gold-foiled bottle and two flutes.

'Champagne?' Selena asked incredulously. *Another first.* 'What is there to celebrate?'

'As yet, nothing.' He shrugged. 'So let us toast a beginning. The launch, if you wish, of our quest and its ultimate success.'

She could hardly refuse, even though she felt out of her depth, caught in some swift, disturbing current that she ought to resist.

The wine was cool, crisp and tingling against her dry throat, as other waiters began to bring plates and a dish containing some kind of green vegetable like small fat cigars.

'*Dolmades,*' her companion told her as they were served. 'Vine leaves stuffed with lamb, rice and herbs.'

Warily, she sampled a bit, then, surprised and delighted, another larger mouthful, savouring the various flavours, and saw him smiling at her.

'Good?'

She nodded. 'Wonderful.'

As was the grilled swordfish with sauté potatoes and salad which followed. And, of course, the champagne, its bubbles seeming to dance along her senses.

The dessert was just right, too—a bowl of fruit to share—peaches, and marvellously sweet figs that he told her had come that day from the garden at the family villa.

'You must have a lot of trees,' she commented, glancing at the now-crowded dining room.

'They are not for everyone. I had them brought specially to welcome you to Greece.'

She flushed. '*Efharisto*, Mr Constantinou.'

'*Parakalo,*' he returned. 'And must we be so formal? As I have told you, my name is Alexis.'

'I think formality is best,' she said. 'Under the circumstances.'

'Even though you will be spending tonight in my bed?' His question was soft and her flush deepened hectically as she struggled for composure.

She said jerkily, 'Please stop saying things like that. In Britain, it could be considered harassment.'

'But now you are in Greece,' he said with a shrug. 'And I have only spoken the truth, unless you plan to sleep on a sofa or the floor.' He paused. 'Tell me something. Why did you not come on holiday with your sister?'

'I had a vacation job. Besides, she was coming with her friends.'

'And your parents permitted this?'

She bit her lip. 'My parents were killed in a car accident. Our aunt acts as our guardian and though she wasn't keen on the holiday at first, she was persuaded by one of the mothers that they'd be fine on such a small island.'

'Yet human nature is the same everywhere. And you had to give up your job to come here?'

'I'd already done so. My aunt tripped in the garden and broke her leg and needed me at home.'

'So how does she manage without you now?' He was frowning.

'She's paying someone,' Selena said shortly. 'Now may I ask you something?'

'If you wish.'

'How is it you speak such good English?'

'My mother was born in America. Although she came to Greece to give birth to me, their only child, she and my father lived mainly in New York, and continued to do so after their divorce when my time was divided between them.'

'That must have been—difficult.'

'Divorce is always hard for children,' he said quietly. 'It is better to deal with mistakes in marriage before they are born.'

She was silent for a moment. Then: 'I suppose in that way we were lucky,' she said slowly. 'My mother and father adored each other and we felt surrounded by happiness. When they were—taken like that, it was dreadful for us, but I've thought since that it was good for them to be together. That if just one had died, the other who was left would never have recovered. They'd have been just part of a person.'

She stopped abruptly, shocked by what she'd said, what she'd let him see—this disturbing stranger that she wasn't even sure she could trust.

She remembered trying to say something similar to Aunt Nora when she was younger, and what the cold reply had been.

'I'm sorry,' she added quickly, trying to force a smile. 'I know that sounds—ridiculously morbid.'

'No,' he said. 'It does not.' He paused. 'Has she been kind to you, this aunt?'

'Yes. Of course.' She straightened her shoulders, silencing inner voices, drawing down mental blinds. 'It can't have been easy for her to be saddled with two pre-adolescents, but she's coped wonderfully.'

He inclined his head politely. 'So wonderfully that your sister cannot wait to escape, whatever the means.'

'My sister,' she said, 'as you've admitted, has been seduced by a serial womaniser, and is probably, and quite naturally, scared of the repercussions.' She added, 'We live in a small town and there's bound to be unpleasant gossip, so I'm here for damage limitation, not to burden you with our family history.'

'It is not a burden.' He signalled to a waiter. 'I suggest that after coffee, you go up to the flat and get some sleep. You have had a long and worrying day, and to-morrow the search truly begins.'

'Thank you,' she said. 'But I think I'll sleep better without coffee.' She rose, and he, too, got to his feet. 'Goodnight, Mr Constantinou.'

'*Kalinichta*, Kyria Blake.' His smile was tinged with irony. 'Until tomorrow, then. Sleep well.'

He didn't add 'in my bed' this time but he might as well have done, Selena thought mutinously as she made her way across the dining room.

And knew, if she looked back, as she had no intention of doing, she would find him watching her go.

Her laundry finished, Selena removed it from the tumble dryer and folded it with care, aware that her hands were shaking.

I should have left the next morning, she told herself for the thousandth time. Got up early and slipped away, leaving a note at the desk, thanking him and saying I'd decided to pursue my own enquiries.

Instead, there she'd been, back in the restaurant, breakfasting on fresh orange juice, warm rolls with honey, and a pot of strong filter coffee, staring through the windows at the sunlight dancing on the water. And forbidding herself to look round every time the faint squeak of the double doors announced a new arrival.

But when her meal was over without any sign of Alexis Constantinou, she was at a loss what to do next.

Perhaps he'd had second thoughts about helping her, she told herself. After all, he had a hotel to run. So she would simply revert to Plan A: go to the police and risk the gossip mill alerting Millie and her boyfriend.

But as she walked out into the foyer, he was waiting for her by the reception desk, casual in cream chinos and a black shirt, sleeves rolled to the elbows, and unbuttoned almost to the waist this time, she saw, her throat tightening.

'*Kalimera.*' His dark glance appraised her own white cut-offs and navy tunic top, then rested briefly on her hair, once more deliberately plaited into a long braid and hanging down her slender back. But he made no comment. 'Did you sleep well?'

'Yes,' she said, adding awkwardly, 'Thank you.'

'And you have eaten, so we can go.' Briskly, he ushered her out of the hotel and through the garden to a Jeep, waiting at the gate.

She hung back. 'Go where?'

'To find Adoni Mandaki, a local fisherman who is also a friend of Kostas.' He handed her into the Jeep, then swung himself into the driver's seat and started the engine. 'I heard in a bar last night that his boat is missing, but he himself has been seen in the town, drinking and playing *tavli* as if its absence did not disturb him, and he has no living to earn.'

'A boat.' Selena bit her lip. 'Do you think Kostas and Millie have left Rhymnos?'

'That is what I hope he will tell us,' he said as they drove down the hill towards the harbour.

She said slowly, 'So, after you sent me to bed, you came down here asking questions about my sister. It didn't occur to you that I might want to be there to hear the answers? And maybe ask some questions of my own?'

He shot her a swift glance. 'It occurred,' he said. 'But I dismissed it.'

'Ignoring the fact that I had a right to be there.'

'To do what? To shout at everyone in English until they told you what you wanted to hear?' His mouth twisted. 'Believe me, it would not have worked. And I decided you needed a night's rest.'

She stiffened. 'Then maybe you'd consult me in future before making any more arbitrary decisions.'

'I will try to remember. In return, perhaps you will now agree to call me Alexis. And tell me your name also.'

'Why is that necessary?'

He shrugged a shoulder. 'Because it suggests that we are on—friendly terms.'

Selena stiffened. 'I think it might imply rather more than that,' she said icily.

'So, people will see me spending a day in the sun with a pretty tourist,' he countered. 'What of it? Once we have found your sister, you will persuade her to leave with you and go, and that will be the end of it.'

He paused. 'Surely that is worth the temporary inconvenience of my company?'

She said reluctantly, 'You make me sound very ungrateful.'

'No,' he said. 'I think you are frightened, and you have reason. It is no easy thing you have been asked to do—to come all this way to a strange country and alone, when you cannot speak the language and do not know where to look.'

He sighed abruptly. 'I see this and I should have

more patience. And perhaps you could try to trust me. Believe that I wish to help you.'

'Yes,' she said. 'Thank you—Alexis.' She hesitated. 'And my name is Selena.'

'Selena,' he repeated, his brows lifting. 'In our language Selene—the goddess of the moon.'

'But people usually call me Lena,' she added hastily.

'Sacrilege,' he said softly. 'For a girl with hair the colour of moonlight.'

She felt an inner jolt as if she'd missed a step downwards. Knew, too, that she was blushing. 'And Millie's really Amelia,' she went on, aware that she was babbling. 'Perhaps she's named after a goddess, too.'

'Alas, no,' he said. 'But maybe to Kostas, she is Aphrodite herself. We shall soon find out.'

'I hope so.' And she meant it.

Because, as she'd suddenly realised, however scared she might be for Millie, she, too, was in danger, with an equally urgent need to get away.

# CHAPTER FOUR

YET NOW HERE she was—once more flying to Millie's rescue, she thought wryly, as, back at the house, she began her packing. But this time the situation was very different, because she would be spared the agonising possibility of encountering Alexis again.

As Kostas had confirmed, he had indeed gone for ever, as she'd been told in that horrifying interview all those months ago.

And now, surely, she could begin to look to a future with hope, not regret.

God, what a fool I was, she thought bitterly, extracting a folder of photographs from a drawer, and tucking one of them into her bag. 'Trust me,' he said, and I was naïve enough to believe him.

And telling herself that, at the time, she'd had little choice was no excuse.

Because, even as they drove along the quayside that first morning in search of Adoni, she could have said she'd changed her mind and requested him to take her to the police station instead.

But she didn't because she was already starting to flounder in a maelstrom of unaccustomed emotions.

At the same time, the bustle at the harbour held its own fascination, too. The air still held the aroma of last night's charcoal grills. The *caiques* were unloading their first catches amid shouting and laughter. Owners of souvenir and clothing shops were unrolling awnings and bringing out their display stands, and at the *tavernas*, cloths were being anchored to the tables with plastic clips, tiled floors hosed down and tubs of geraniums watered.

As the Jeep went past, people called smiling greetings to Alexis, who waved in acknowledgement.

Like a royal progress, Selena thought with faint amusement.

'Do you always get this kind of reception?' she asked.

He shrugged. 'Only when I have been away for a while. Many of those who live here regard the world outside Rhymnos as a dangerous place and are glad to see I have returned safely, and that all is as it should be again.' He shot her a swift glance. 'You find that strange?'

'I find everything about this situation strange,' she returned tautly.

'Yet you will soon accustom yourself, I promise.'

But I don't want to become used to this place—this way of life, she thought, her throat tightening. I can't afford that.

They reached a dilapidated warehouse, hardly more than a shack, its doors standing open. Deftly, Alexis slotted the Jeep between two trucks on the other side of the road, and switched off the engine.

'Adoni sleeps here sometimes when he is not on his boat,' he said. 'Wait here while I see if he is sober enough to talk.'

'I want to come with you,' Selena protested.

'But I wish you to stay where you are,' he said softly. 'I have my reasons.'

Which of course take precedence, she thought resentfully watching his tall figure stride across the road and disappear into the dark interior of the building.

Unless she was there, how could she be sure he'd ask the right questions?

On the other hand, she had no real wish to encounter a Greek fisherman with a hangover.

There was a haze over the sea and the heat was building steadily. It was going to be a scorching day, she thought, pulling off her broad-brimmed cotton sunhat and using it languidly to fan herself.

Her thin tunic was already clinging to her damp skin, and she was just hoping that Alexis's interrogation would not take too long or she might melt, when he emerged from the shack accompanied by another man, stout, bearded and clad only in a pair of sagging shorts.

Some Adonis, she thought critically.

However, he appeared to be doing all the talking, and was smiling at the same time, which might be a good sign, while Alexis stood, head bent, listening.

As she watched, she suddenly realised that she, too, was under scrutiny. That Adoni had spotted her and was staring openly, his smile broadening into a grin as he made some comment to Alexis.

Then they both laughed, clapped each other on the shoulder, and Alexis walked back to the Jeep.

As he swung himself into the driving seat, he turned

to her, shrugging and spreading his hands almost rue-fully.

'Look disappointed, Selene *mou*,' he whispered urgently. 'Pout a little.'

'Disappointed?' she echoed, staring at him appalled.

Had Adoni refused to help—pleaded ignorance? Had they come so soon to a dead end?

As her thoughts rampaged, Alexis reached out a hand and clasped the nape of her neck, his fingers lightly stroking the silky skin under the pale blonde braid.

Taken totally by surprise, she felt her pulses leap and the quivering ache of an unfamiliar tremor along her senses. In sudden panic, she tried to push him away, but she was too late. He was already drawing her towards him, pulling her against him, imprisoning her hands between their bodies, holding her helpless, while his mouth took her parted, outraged lips in a long and very thorough kiss.

A kiss for which nothing in her life so far could possibly have prepared her.

She was conquered, consumed by the pressure of his mouth moving on her, enjoying her, by his clean breath sighing into hers and the heated intimate glide of his tongue against her own.

Half drugged by the heat of the sun, its golden clamour against her closed eyelids and the warm, male scent of his skin, she found herself prey to feelings—to needs she had not known existed until that moment.

She thought dazedly: I have to make him stop.

And then: I never want him to stop.

Because something—some sensation was uncurling deep inside her, sending out little tendrils of pleasure that were beginning to bloom and grow and which, instinct warned her, could easily overwhelm her.

And then suddenly, with a shock as brutal as a slap across the face, she was free, and Alexis was sitting back at a decorous distance watching her, his expression unfathomable.

He said coolly, 'I hope I have not caused permanent damage to your hat, *agapi mou*.'

Numbly, she looked down at it, crushed in her hand, and suddenly her predominant emotion was shame that she'd allowed him to—maul her in full view of anyone who cared to look. And although he had certainly not been brutal, her mouth felt hot. Swollen.

'You.' Her voice almost choked as her hands clenched into belated fists. 'How *dare* you...'

'Be calm.' He held her wrists, fending her off with the utmost ease. There was a note of laughter in his voice. 'As I thought I made clear, I want Adoni to see you disappointed, Selene *mou*, not dangerous.'

'You *wanted* him to watch that—that disgusting performance?'

'I wanted him to watch you being consoled for the loss of our romantic trip together in the seclusion of his boat.'

'But—the boat is supposed to be missing.'

'Why, yes,' he said. 'As he explained when I suggested hiring it for the day. I was too late, he told me. A friend had already borrowed it—for his honeymoon.'

'Honeymoon,' Selena repeated dazedly. 'You mean that Kostas and Millie are married?'

He sighed. 'No, I merely changed the words he really used in order to spare your blushes.'

'Oh,' Selena said and began to smooth the creases out of her hat, her fingers all thumbs. She swallowed. 'And you let him think that you—that I...'

'Wished to share the same delight,' he supplied courteously as she stumbled to a halt.

'Did he actually say it was Kostas who'd borrowed his boat?' She jumped to safer ground.

'No,' he said. 'Because he knows that Kostas should be working at the hotel not off somewhere enjoying his new lover, and assumes that his absence has not been reported to me. A real beauty, he told me. Such golden hair, such eyes. A hot little English honey.'

'Oh.' Selena bent her head, covering her face with her hands. 'Oh, God.'

He said, 'If you are going to weep, Selene *mou*, can you wait until we have more privacy? I do not want the whole of Rhymnos to think I ill-treat you.'

She straightened defiantly, glaring at him. 'I have no intention of crying. I'm too angry. How do you think it makes me feel—hearing that Millie's been discussed— leered over like that—when she doesn't deserve it?' She took a breath. 'Because whatever Daisy and Fiona may have done, she wouldn't have been involved. I know it.'

He was silent for a moment, then he said quite gently, 'You are at university, *ne*? And in the vacations, you work.'

'Most students do.' She was defensive.

'So you have not always been there to see, perhaps, that she has changed. That maybe she is no longer the little sister—the child of the family. That she has grown up—spread her wings.'

Selena gasped. 'What are you saying?' she demanded. 'That she chased Kostas—not the other way round? That she's the one to blame for all this?'

He sighed. 'No, Selene *mou*. That is not what I mean. Just that the situation may not be as clear-cut as you believe.' He started the engine. 'But first we must find them, and do so quickly. Adoni tells me there is going to be a storm.'

And as she glanced up incredulously at the cloudless sky, he added drily, 'And where the weather is concerned, at least, he is never wrong.'

Almost as soon as the harbour was left behind, the road became little more than a rutted track, with the sea on one side and a scatter of small single storey houses on the other, their gardens neatly tended, with chickens pecking in the dust and the occasional goat tethered on the verge.

And behind them, stretching away towards the grey and amethyst rocks crowning the hills in the centre of the island, the ancient twisted trunks of olive trees, their leaves shimmering like silver in the sunlight.

'Don't the locals complain about this surface?' Selena asked, grabbing the side of the Jeep after one particularly severe jolt.

'Not that I have heard. Besides their transport is accustomed to it,' he added, indicating two donkeys peacefully browsing in the shade of a tree.

She said in a hollow voice, 'Oh, I see.'

'I think you are beginning to.' There was faint amusement in his voice, and she flushed.

'I can't help it if things seem strange. I haven't been abroad before.'

'And even now it is business, not pleasure, that brings you—and alone.' He paused pointedly. 'To me, that is strange.'

'But hardly my choice,' she returned coolly. And let him make what he would of that.

'So,' she went on, 'where are we going?'

'To look for Adoni's boat. Where else?'

'But it could be anywhere.'

'I think not. It is hardly a luxury yacht,' he added drily. 'Nor is it equipped for a long voyage. So it is probable they have moored where they can have access to a beach and some form of shelter, and on Rhymnos such places are few.'

He shot her a swift sideways glance. 'Try to relax, Selene *mou*. We will find them, and soon, I promise you.'

She nodded. She said in a stifled voice, 'I keep thinking this is all a bad dream and that, in a minute, I'm going to wake up back in Haylesford with Millie asleep in the next room.'

'Truly? Is this place where you live so dear to you?'

No, she thought. And it never will be. But right now it represents a kind of security.

She said quickly, 'Of course. It's my home.' And paused. 'You must feel the same about Rhymnos.'

There was an odd silence, then he said almost harshly, 'Yes, I do.'

She looked at him, startled at his tone, then by the sudden starkness she saw in his face and the grim set of his mouth.

Was shocked to find herself wanting to put her hand on his arm. To say, *Tell me what's wrong. What's troubling you...?*

And thought that she must be going crazy, because, in reality, that was the last thing in the world that she needed to do.

Keep your distance, she warned herself urgently. Be polite now, grateful when you get Millie back, and leave it at that.

She turned slightly, staring at the sea, noticing that it had become smoother, like a sheet of glass, and that a ridge of pale cloud seemed to be building on the horizon.

It looked as if Adoni's prediction about the weather was coming true after all, she thought uneasily, transferring her attention to the olive groves clustering on the other side of the track.

She said, trying to sound like an interested tourist, 'People must use a lot of olive oil.'

'They use what they need,' he said. 'Most of it now goes for export.'

'From a tiny place like this?' She was astounded.

'Yes,' he said. 'Until quite recently, each household gathered and pressed its own olives and stored the oil. But it was felt they deserved a wider market, so the islanders were persuaded to join a co-operative and now their olives are collected and processed at a new, modern plant on the other side of the island and sold worldwide under the Rhymnos label.'

Selena's eyes widened. 'I think it's on sale in the supermarket near the university. Do the bottles have a picture of three stone columns?'

He smiled faintly. 'The pillars of Apollo, all, sadly, that remains of his ancient temple.' He paused. 'I shall be happy to show it to you.'

'I'm afraid there won't be time,' she said quickly. 'Millie and I have to return to the UK on the first available flight.'

'Of course,' he said. 'In the pleasure of your company, Selene *mou*, I had almost forgotten.'

She reverted hastily to the safer topic of olive oil. 'Was it you who persuaded the islanders to join this co-operative, by any chance?'

'I was not alone,' he said. 'Our priest, Father Stephanos, supported the scheme, and most of the headmen of the villages, who knew fishing and tourism would not make Rhymnos self-sufficient. And fortunately, I had contacts in the States in advertising, as well as marketing and distribution, which I could offer as an incentive.'

His smile was rueful. 'But it was not easy. The idea of a co-operative held little appeal at first. Now they can take pride in its success.'

And they're grateful, too, Selena thought. It explains the royal progress earlier. And maybe it means that I can trust him, that it's good to have him on my side, even if his main concern is the good name of his hotel rather than Millie.

The journey proceeded in silence, Alexis driving steadily, scanning the sea as they went. It now looked like burnished steel, she saw uneasily, and the sky had almost disappeared behind a grey veil, through which the sun's disc burned with a sullen orange.

At the same time, she realised that the Jeep was slowing. Alexis pulled over on to the rough grass at the side of the track and parked in the shade of yet another olive tree.

She craned her neck to look past it. 'Have you seen the boat?'

He looked at her, frowning slightly. 'No, but this is the only other place where they could have come ashore, and there is a good, dry cave. If they are using it, they may intend to return. There may be signs of this, so I am going down to check.'

Selena scrambled out. 'I'll come with you.'

His frown deepened. 'You would do better to stay here,' he advised brusquely. 'The path is difficult.'

'Do you think I care?' She confronted him, chin lifted. 'If there's anything in that cave, I—I want to see it.'

There was a brief, taut pause, then he said quietly, 'Whatever horrors you are imagining, *agapi mou*, put them out of your head. The most I expect to see is water—the remains of food—perhaps a blanket.'

'It makes no difference. I want to look for myself.'

When she saw how steep the route to the beach really was, she began to regret her intransigence, and when Alexis paused at the edge of the cliff and silently extended his hand, she took it without demur.

Their descent was slow and wary, and she found it was better to concentrate on the loose stones threatening to roll away under her feet than to look down at the beach.

When they finally reached the foot of the cliff, she re-alised she'd been holding her breath and, as she released it with a gasp, wondered if that was due to the gradi-ent or more to the firm clasp of his fingers round hers.

Releasing herself, she said quickly, 'I don't see any cave.'

He pointed to a huge boulder. 'The entrance is be-hind there.'

He strode off across the beach, and she followed more awkwardly, her feet sinking in the coarse, gritty sand. An apprehensive look upwards told her that the overcast of cloud had now blotted out the sun com-pletely.

It had become very still, as if the world around them was waiting. Gathering itself. That she and Alexis were all that moved in a silent landscape, and she suddenly remembered the saying, 'The calm before the storm.'

As she reached the rock, she paused as she saw the narrow entrance it was guarding and the darkness be-yond.

She'd never experienced even mild claustrophobia, but there had to be a first time for everything, and in spite of the oppressive heat, she felt a quick shiver run down her spine.

At the same moment, she glimpsed a jagged flash over the sea, followed by a sullen rumble of thunder and the first few heavy drops of rain, sharp and cold against her skin.

Alexis was gesturing at her impatiently from the opening to the cave. 'Come quickly,' he called. 'Run.'

As she reached him, he took her by the shoulders,

turned her sideways and thrust her through the gap, following immediately behind her as outside the rain was gathering to a deluge.

It was dim in the cave, but, as her eyes adjusted, she realised that after the cramped entrance had been negotiated, it opened out quite astonishingly, its roof well over six feet high at the front, allowing Alexis to stand upright, but tapering down to less than four feet at the rear. However, it was also completely empty.

Her voice shook with disappointment. 'They haven't been here.'

Another jagged flash tore at the sky outside, bathing the cave for an instant in a strange green light.

Alexis said something under his breath and bent to the sandy floor. When he straightened, a short length of heavy silver links was dangling from his fingers.

He said, 'Someone has—and not so long ago, or this would have been hidden by the sand.' He looked at her. 'You know this?'

Selena stared at the broken chain, her throat tightening. She said huskily, 'It's the bracelet I bought Millie for Christmas,' flinching as another crack of thunder echoed around them.

As it died away, he said, 'Then you had better take it,' and dropped it into her hand.

She pushed it into her pants pocket. 'So she was here—with him. Oh, where are they? What has he done with her?'

There was another violent flash of eerie green light and then, almost at once and right above their heads, an ominous rumble building slowly and inexorably to a roaring, deafening crash as if the entire cliff was collapsing on top of them.

Selena cried out, her voice lost in the uproar, and stumbled forward, her hands reaching out to Alexis, who caught her and held her, wrapped closely in his arms, his hand stroking her hair, until the last terrifying echoes of the thunder died away, and all she could hear was the tumultuous thud of her own heartbeat.

And, beneath her cheek, his—like the relentless rhythm of a drum.

He lifted his head and stood for a long moment, unmoving, giving her the odd sensation that the entire world had suddenly shrunk to the circle of his arms and that, once again, it was waiting in breathless anticipation.

That she herself was poised—on the edge of some momentous discovery, her whole being suffused by a warm and unfamiliar languor.

His hand moved down, brushing a few damp strands of hair from her temples, then tracing her cheek and the delicate line of her jaw with his fingertips. Impelling her silently to look up at him. To read his intention in the sudden flare of his gaze as he bent and his mouth found hers, gently, sensuously coaxing her lips to part for him.

She leaned into the heat and strength of his body, this time welcoming his kiss, responding with bewildered ardour as it deepened, and a shiver of pleasure feathered enticingly across her skin.

His hands slid down her body to clasp her hips and pull her even closer, making her frankly aware of his arousal, and, to her shocked astonishment, of the heated, melting ache of her own needs. Unguessed-at, perhaps, unbidden—certainly, but frighteningly potent just the same, turning her suddenly into a stranger to herself.

When, at last, he took his lips slowly from hers, she made a small, lost sound in her throat that never became an actual word, even if she'd been able to think of one.

She lifted her shaking hands and pushed aside the edges of his shirt, her fingers tracing the uncompromising line of his shoulders before they drifted down to discover his muscular torso and the way it clenched under her untutored touch.

His hands were moving, too, swift and deft as he unfastened the buttons that closed her tunic and slipped it down, baring her to the waist. He cupped her rounded breasts in his palms, his fingertips teasing her nipples into hard and aching peaks, then drew her against him, grazing them with his hair-roughened chest until she could have cried out with the delight that pierced her to the core of her womanhood, that made her burn and melt.

As if the body she had fed and clothed but never been remotely tempted to share with anyone had taken on a life and purpose of its own, fierce and unrecognisable.

That showed her, at last, the mystery of desire.

But not, she realised dazedly, its answer.

Because the hands that held her, although still gentle, were putting her away from him. Distancing her.

Isolated on the other side of the space between them, she saw those same caressing hands ball into fists and become hidden in the pockets of his chinos. Watched the muscles move in his throat as he swallowed.

He said quietly and harshly, 'This—should not have happened. Forgive me.'

For an instant, she was transfixed, knowing there was nothing to forgive. That wherever he had led, she would have gladly followed. That he must have known that.

Yet he had still turned away.

Pride came to her rescue, and the self-containment that the past nine years had taught her. She turned her back, pulling her top back into place, fumbling with the buttons.

She said over her shoulder, 'I should apologise, too. I—I'm not usually afraid of thunder, but I thought the roof was going to collapse and I—panicked.'

In the part of her mind still functioning on the rim of reality, she registered that the crackle of the lightning had become less frequent and the answering thunder had become a sullen mumble in the distance.

She added, with a kind of ludicrous brightness, 'But at least the storm is over.'

There was an odd silence, then he said quietly, 'On the contrary, Selene *mou*, I think it is just beginning.' He paused again. 'Now let us resume our search.'

And he led the way out of the cave and back to the Jeep.

# CHAPTER FIVE

BEHAVE AS IF it didn't happen, she told herself repeatedly as she scrambled back up the cliff, this time without assistance. Or as if it was just a random incident to be shrugged away and forgotten.

Back on level ground, she paused, shading her eyes against the emergence of a watery sun and staring out to sea as if she could conjure up Adoni's boat by sheer force of will. Then, her breathing under control, she followed Alexis over to the Jeep.

When she arrived, she found that he'd produced a towel from somewhere and was using it to wipe away the rain that had gathered on the front seats.

'So, where do we go from here?' She gestured towards the Aegean, keeping her tone brisk. 'If they're just sailing around, how can we possibly trace them?'

'By helicopter, perhaps.' He screwed up the damp towel and tossed it in the back of the Jeep.

'Helicopter,' she repeated and managed a short laugh. 'Now why didn't I think of that? And I suppose you have one available?'

'Of course.' His glance was sardonic. 'Or I would not have suggested it. It is at my house.'

She absorbed that with a gulp. 'You didn't think of using that first?'

'Yes,' he said. 'But I decided, wrongly it seems, that tracking them this way would be a simple matter.'

'Maybe you don't know Kostas as well as you thought.'

'I will not,' he said softly, 'make the obvious remark about your sister, Selene *mou*.'

Her search for a crushing retort was halted as she realised he was stripping off his shirt.

'What—what are you doing?'

'Making sure you are comfortable for the rest of our trip.' He folded the shirt into a neat pad and put it on the still-damp passenger seat. 'Shall we go?'

He was about to start the engine when there was a loud trill from the mobile phone in the well between the seats.

He answered it brusquely, then listened for a moment, his expression, she saw, changing from impatience to incredulity. Then he barked off a response and switched off the phone, sitting in silence for a moment, staring through the windshield.

She said, 'Has something happened?'

'Why, yes, *agapi mou*.' He started the Jeep. 'It seems that we shall not need the helicopter after all. Adoni's boat is back in the harbour and Kostas and your sister are now at my house, together with his mother, who shares your views about their relationship and has been saying so very loudly.' His lip curled. 'My staff have had a dramatic morning.'

She bit her lip. 'I—I'm sorry.'

She could only hope that all this signalled the parting of the ways and that Millie would be glad to put Rhymnos and its mistakes behind her and go quietly back to England.

And she won't be the only one, she reminded herself without pleasure.

He said, 'I thought you would be jubilant.'

She looked down at her hands, clenched together in her lap. 'I'm just trying to figure out what to say to them both.'

'You have only to talk to your sister,' he said, adding with a touch of grimness, 'I shall deal with Kostas. And his mother.'

'Oh,' she said. 'Well—thank you.' She paused. 'Millie—and Kostas. Do they still seem to be speaking to each other?'

'Speaking, holding hands and refusing to be parted, also loudly. Not, I think, what you wanted to hear.' He glanced at her frowningly. 'You were hoping she would simply leave without an argument?'

'Well, naturally.'

'You are an optimist, Selene *mou*.' He paused. 'So— let us speak of your aunt. Clearly, she has money. How much do you think she would be willing to pay for your sister's return?'

'You mean—Kostas might be bought?'

'Who knows?' His tone was cynical. 'But, in the end, money tends to speak louder than words of love.'

Selena bit her lip. She said quietly, 'I doubt she'd even consider it.'

'And, in that event, what awaits your sister in England?'

'School. Some important exam results. College interviews.' She saw his mouth twist and added hastily, 'Oh, and her eighteenth birthday in a few weeks' time.'

'A few weeks,' he repeated softly. '*Po, po, po.* Then you do not have much time,' he added and put his foot down hard on the accelerator.

She was braced for another bone-shaking trip, but almost at once found they were joining a broad, level road, apparently of recent construction and cutting across the middle of the island. It was a bleak landscape consisting mainly of wide stretches of stone and scrub and dominated by the huddle of rugged hills at the centre and hardly, she thought, justifying an access like this.

Until she saw they were approaching a collection of single storey buildings, composed of concrete blocks and corrugated iron, enclosed by a high wire fence, with a large sign at the entrance displaying three golden pillars.

'Oh,' she said. 'Is that where the olive oil is produced?'

'*Ne.*' He slanted a smile at her. 'Not beautiful, I agree. But efficient.'

'Is that why it's here—in the middle of nowhere?'

He tutted reprovingly. 'Rhymnos,' he said, 'is too small to have a nowhere. Everything is close to somewhere. In this case—where a dream became an idea and the idea moved to reality.'

'I'm not very good at riddles.'

He shrugged a shoulder. 'If you were staying, I could explain.'

She kept her voice light. 'As it is, I shall just have to live with my curiosity.'

'And so,' he said softly, 'shall I.'

A comment she deemed it wiser not to pursue.

The road stretched out in front of them, winding its way round the bottom of the hills, the barren landscape giving way to more olive groves, but interspersed now with well-kept orchards growing lemons, peaches and figs.

And beyond them, at last, standing alone in its spacious grounds was the Villa Helios, a sprawl of white stone, topped with faded green roof tiles and set against the coruscating blue of the sea.

Now *that*, thought Selena, catching her breath, that *is* beautiful. She was aware of Alexis shooting her a sideways glance and smiling as he interpreted her reaction.

He drove round to the rear of the villa and parked in a yard where chickens scattered, clucking indignantly at the intrusion.

Selena followed him to an open doorway, bracing herself as they walked down a passage lined with store and laundry rooms to another door leading straight into a large kitchen, seemingly crowded with people.

For a moment there was silence, then, just as Selena had registered that Millie was not one of the crowd, this was hideously broken by a series of piercing shrieks from a thin woman clad in funereal black from her headscarf to her shoes, who was seated at the massive central table.

Selena took an involuntary step backwards, stumbling a little, and felt herself caught and steadied by Alexis's hands on her shoulders. Immediately the screeches increased in volume and a middle-aged woman in a neat grey dress came forward spreading her hands in a kind of helpless embarrassment, murmuring in Greek. She was plump, her dark hair streaked with grey and drawn into a bun on top of her head. Her round face suggested that her expression was usually merry and that her black eyes would twinkle, given the opportunity. Only they weren't twinkling now.

Alexis said something quiet and savage, half under his breath, then crooked an imperative finger to summon a young girl in a maid's uniform.

'Go with Penelope to your sister, Selene,' he directed. 'I will join you when I have spoken to Kostas.'

Selena found herself guided out of another door and down a short passage into an impressive entrance hall and across to a pair of double doors. As the girl reached to open them, Selena halted her. 'Do you speak English...er... Penelope?'

'*Ne, thespinis.* When I was a child, I lived in America.'

'Then can you tell me why that woman started screaming when we arrived?'

Penelope's pretty face was lit by a swift smile. 'Madame Papoulis is very devout—very modest, *thespinis.* She was offended that Kyrios Alexis was not wearing a shirt.'

Selena's eyes widened. 'But she's been married,' she exclaimed. 'Surely she can't be that shocked.'

Penelope shrugged. 'There are many kinds of marriage, *thespinis*. Maybe we should pity her husband, *ne*?'

And on that, she ushered Selena into the room beyond.

'What are you doing here?' was Millie's defensive greeting as the door closed behind Selena.

Her face mutinous and unsmiling, she was perched on the edge of a sofa, clad in tiny white shorts and a skimpy black bikini bra, her finger and toe nails lacquered gold.

'And hello to you, too,' Selena returned equably. 'I came to see if you were all right.'

Millie hunched a shoulder, putting the bra top in peril. 'Of course I am. Didn't Daisy and Fiona pass on my message?'

'Such as it was.' *Don't lose your temper. Just walk to a chair and sit down.* 'Didn't it occur to you that Aunt Nora would be worried sick?'

'Worried, no,' Millie returned calmly. 'Mad as fire, yes. However, I've now written to her, explaining everything, and asking her to send my birth certificate and some other stuff. Will you make sure she does it?'

'Your birth certificate?' Selena stared at her. 'Why?'

'Because I'll need it to get married as soon as I'm eighteen. Greek law.'

'Married?'

*Oh, God*, thought Selena. *I sound like an echo. And that's why Alexis said there was no time to be lost.*

She took a deep breath. 'Millie, for heaven's sake, think what you're doing. You're throwing away your future...'

'On the contrary, my future is going to be with the man I love.'

'Someone you hardly know.'

'I knew within the first hour. So did he,' Millie said defiantly. 'You may be content to slave away for our beloved aunt for the rest of your life, but I want something different. Something better. And I'm taking it.'

And if she means it, thought Selena, with a sudden, joyous lift of the heart, then I'm also off the hook.

She said slowly, 'I had my reasons for doing what Aunt Nora wanted, but now they no longer apply. So, let's get back to you. Do you really imagine you can both live on what Kostas earns from seasonal bar work?'

'I can work, too. Besides, he won't always be just a barman,' Millie said defiantly. 'He has ambition. He's going to have his own *taverna*.'

'But until then, where will you live?'

'Well—at the hotel.' For the first time there was a note of uncertainty in her sister's voice. 'Of course, Kostas will have to clear it with his boss, but that shouldn't be a problem. And I can be—a chambermaid or something,' she added with a vague gesture.

Bold talk from someone normally incapable of making her own bed, Selena thought cynically.

She said, 'I wouldn't count on it, Mills. If there are any staff vacancies, they'll almost certainly be offered to local people.'

She paused. 'Anyway, you're so young to be making this kind of decision. You need to see more of life—meet other men—before you settle down.'

'Oh, for heaven's sake, Lena.' Her sister sighed. 'I'm

not a virgin, and I've been on the pill since I was six-teen, so I probably know more about "life", as you put it, than you do.

'I came out here to have a good time with a couple of mates and I certainly didn't expect to fall in love. Nor did Kostas, let me tell you. But it happened, and what-ever you think, it ain't going to change.

'And I'm relying on you to get Aunt Nora on side,' she added. 'After all, you'll be the blue-eyed girl from now on. Make her see I'm entitled to live my own life.'

At the same time curing world hunger I suppose, Selena thought despairingly.

As she tried to marshal her arguments for another attempt, there was a rap at the door and Alexis walked in, once again fully clad, and trailed by a young man, who, in spite of his sulky expression, still managed to be spectacularly good looking with the build of a Hollywood action hero.

Selena could see the attraction, but was far from reassured.

'Kostas. Darling.' Millie jumped up and hurled her-self at him. 'Is everything fixed?'

'*Ochi*. No, *kougla mou*.' He sighed. 'Kyrios Alexis says that you should return to England with your sister.'

'But I've already made it clear to her that I'm not leaving Rhymnos.' She turned wide eyes and a pretty smile on Alexis who appeared curiously unmoved.

'Surely you can understand we want to be together and find a little corner for me, while we wait to be mar-ried. I promise that I'll be no trouble.'

Alexis spoke bleakly. 'Forgive me, *thespinis*, but you

have already caused more trouble than you can imagine. The staff accommodation at the hotel is for single occupation only and I make no exceptions. Also your presence may continue to distract Kostas from his work.' He paused. 'You wish him to keep his job, do you not?'

'Yes, of course.' The blue eyes began to swim with tears. 'Why are you being so cruel?'

'Perhaps in order to be kind.' His dark face was harsh. 'Marriage is a serious business and this has not started well. You both need time to think—to reflect. Mistakes once made are not easy to put right.'

'But this is not a mistake.' Kostas turned on him. 'My Amelia is the only woman I shall ever want.' He struck his chest with a clenched fist. 'I cannot live without her.'

Alexis's mouth tightened. 'Very dramatic,' he said coldly. 'Perhaps you should seek work with the National Theatre.' He jerked his head towards the door. 'There is food waiting for you in the dining room. Go and eat while I talk with Kyria Blake.' He paused. 'And you, *thespinis*, should dress in something more discreet before you are seen by your fiancé's mother.'

They went reluctantly, Millie, having apparently abandoned the idea of weeping, sending him a fulminating glance instead.

'So,' Alexis said when they were alone. 'As I feared, you are having problems, Selene *mou*. What will you do now?'

'I don't know.' Selena bit her lip. 'I can hardly force her to the aircraft, kicking and screaming. I suppose I should really talk to my aunt.'

He pointed to a side table. 'The telephone is at your disposal. You know the code?'

'Yes,' she said. 'Thank you.'

'Then I will leave you to make your call.' At the door, he turned. 'I wish you luck, *agapi mou*.'

She was sitting on the sofa Millie had vacated, gazing unseeingly into space, when he came to look for her some ten minutes later.

'The conversation did not go well.' He was stating a fact, not asking a question, as he scanned her pale face.

'No. She was—furious.' She tried and failed to smile. 'With me even more than Millie, I think.'

*Fool of a girl—completely useless—can't have been trying.*

The words stung at her.

She said, 'I've been told I have to make Millie see sense, however long it takes.' She swallowed. 'And I'm forbidden to go back without her.'

'*Po, po, po.*' He sat down beside her, not touching. 'She has little understanding of love, this aunt.'

'You think it's really that?' she asked wistfully. 'That they genuinely love each other?'

'Who knows?' He shrugged. 'Only time can tell. When I spoke earlier to Kostas, he claimed to care for your sister very deeply. Perhaps it is the first time in his life that he has felt this for a woman.'

Selena sighed. 'All the same, I have to try again to change her mind.'

'But not at once, perhaps,' he said musingly. 'Let them think that you have accepted the situation, and that you are only staying on to give your aunt's anger time to cool.'

He added, 'Who knows? If they are no longer persecuted lovers, their romance may lose some of its excitement, especially if passion is exchanged for convention.'

He paused. 'Tell me—can your sister cook? Clean a house? Look after hens—even milk a goat?'

She stared at him. 'Millie? Of course not.'

'Then for Kostas's sake, she must learn,' he said briskly. 'I will have your belongings brought from the hotel, Selene *mou*. You and your sister will stay here as my guests. My housekeeper will act as chaperone when Kostas comes to visit your sister. Eleni has a fierce reputation,' he added drily. 'So he will attempt no further liberties.'

He paused. 'And your sister will spend time each day with my staff, learning to cook and clean.'

She drew an incredulous breath. 'Millie will never agree to all this.'

'I think she will, *agapi mou*, when it is explained to her that this is the path that leads to her wedding.'

He added softly, 'I shall also suggest that Father Stephanos gives her instruction in the Greek Orthodox faith, which may soften the attitude of Kostas's mother to the marriage.'

Ridiculously, she found herself bristling. 'Why should she object?'

'Because she will already have picked out a suitable bride for her only son,' he said calmly. 'Does this not happen in England, too?'

'Not where I live. But do whatever you must to stop

her screaming again,' she said reluctantly. 'Although I really don't see the point of encouraging them to get married.'

'This is not encouragement,' he said with a touch of grimness. 'More a demonstration to your sister of what she may expect as the wife of a working man on Rhymnos. Who can say what her reaction to this new regime will be.'

She said slowly, 'You think she'll hate it and want to leave.'

'We can hope. You have a better idea?'

'No,' she admitted reluctantly. 'But once again, you're being put to a great deal of trouble.'

'It's no problem. And while your sister is occupied, you, Selene *mou*, will learn to relax. To be free to swim, and to sunbathe. To drink wine and, I hope, enjoy all that Rhymnos has to offer.'

He got to his feet and walked to the door. 'After all, where else do you have to go?'

And left her staring after him.

With hindsight, she realised how easy it had been. How stupidly, terrifyingly easy to tell herself that she was only agreeing to this for Millie's sake.

That it might only be a week or so before her sister decided she'd had enough of Greek home economics and would prefer to go back to Haylesford.

The time would soon pass, she told herself and when, mission accomplished, she arrived back with Millie, their aunt might, for once, be forced to eat her words.

At least she had to try it and see if it worked.

Upon which, the door re-opened abruptly and the plump woman in grey entered.

She said without preamble, 'I am Eleni Validis, *thespinis*. If you will come with me, I shall show you your room.'

As Selena scrambled to her feet, the housekeeper crossed the room, opened the wide glass doors that almost filled one wall and slid back the shutters beyond, revealing a spacious courtyard with a large swimming pool at its centre.

Skirting the pool in Eleni's brisk wake, Selena felt the heat like a blow.

More shutters, another pair of glass doors and she found herself in a capacious bedroom, with cream walls, matching floor tiles, and filmy cream and gold drapes at the windows. Confronting her was the widest bed she'd ever seen, its snowy linen set off by the midnight blue coverlet folded across its foot.

Facing it, and flanked by an array of louvred wardrobes in pale wood, was an archway leading to a bathroom tiled in glowing mother of pearl.

In the centre of the ceiling, a large fan murmured softly as it turned.

She swallowed and turned to Eleni. 'It's—beautiful. Thank you.' She smiled. 'I mean—*efharisto*.'

But there was no responding smile, just a brief inclination of the head. 'Lunch will be served in an hour, *thespinis*. Yorgos will come to take you to the dining room.' And, on that, she crossed to the door opposite and disappeared into a white-walled passage.

So much for Greek hospitality, thought Selena, feeling a little bleak. But maybe they're accustomed to a better class of visitor and infinitely less aggravation.

Having explored her new domain, she would have dearly loved to cool down in the walk-in shower, or even soak in the deep tub, but was deterred by her lack of clean clothes to change into.

But she soon found an hour was a long time to be alone with one's thoughts—especially when they were as potentially disturbing as hers were becoming.

It was almost a relief when the passage door was flung open and Millie marched in, scowling.

'Kostas has gone,' she announced tragically.

'Gone?' Selena repeated on a note of hope.

'His brute of a boss has taken him back to the hotel.'

'Oh,' said Selena, sighing inwardly as hope died. 'Well, that is where he works.'

'And about as far from this place as it's possible to get,' Millie flung back. 'But if they're hoping to keep us apart, it won't work. Kostas intends to borrow his cousin's motor bike.'

She glanced around, her frown deepening. 'Easy to see who's going to be the skivvy round here. This room is twice the size of mine.'

'If it matters so much, we could swap.'

'What—and disobey the orders of the great god Constantinou?' Millie asked derisively. 'You must be joking. He practically owns the island and everyone in it. They all jump to his bidding.'

'Including you,' Selena said drily, noting the demure blue chambray dress Millie was now wearing. 'Isn't that your school uniform?'

Millie grimaced. 'I wore it to the airport to avoid grief from Aunt Nora. And I thought it might do me some good with Kostas's mother. Fat chance. As soon as she saw me, the old bag started beating her chest with her clenched fists and screaming. You've never heard anything like it.'

That's what you think, Selena informed her silently.

'Kostas brought us here hoping his boss would speak to her for us,' Millie continued angrily. 'Tell her he approved of the marriage. We had no idea she'd got here first.'

Selena said quietly, 'She was probably worried about his disappearance. And maybe the skivvying, as you call it, will be worthwhile if Mrs Papoulis thinks you're trying to learn to be a good Greek wife.'

'I wouldn't bet on it.' Millie paused. 'And why are you still here? Why didn't Mr Constantinou take you back, as well, to pick up your stuff and catch the ferry?'

The million dollar question, thought Selena.

She said carefully, 'Because I'm also trying to avoid grief from Aunt Nora. She's angry because you won't come home with me.'

'Too bad,' said Millie. 'Besides, Rhymnos is my home and I'm not leaving, now or ever, so you're in for a long wait, babes. Enjoy.'

And in a whirl of blue chambray she was gone, leaving Selena standing rigid in the middle of a beautiful room that had suddenly become a trap of her own making.

Or his, she thought. And shivered.

# CHAPTER SIX

LUNCH PROVED TO be a simple affair of grilled chicken with a Greek salad, accompanied by a light and crisp white wine and followed by fresh fruit.

To her surprise, Selena found sheer hunger overcoming her stomach's nervous churning and ate every bite.

'Not exactly a banquet,' Millie commented sourly as they drank the thick, sweet Greek coffee. 'Any more than this place is a mansion,' she added, giving the cool blue-washed dining room a derisive glance. 'And there isn't even an infinity pool. You wouldn't think the Constantinou family were billionaires.'

Selena put down her cup, suddenly breathless as if she'd been kicked in the ribs.

She thought, That's nonsense. He owns a hotel, that's all. Although even that might represent untold riches on such a small island.

And yet…

As if she'd returned to a half-finished puzzle, pieces began to fall into place.

Even if billionaires didn't usually do their own stock-taking, they could find the money to fund roads and olive oil processing plants, and successfully launch a new product in an already thriving market.

Besides, there'd been that casual reference to contacts in the States and, of course, the helicopter as if that mode of transport was the norm.

Not to mention the effortless way he'd taken charge. His assumption that she would follow his advice, allow him to solve her problem and, finally, accept his hospitality.

A powerful man, she realised dazedly. Accustomed to doing exactly what he wanted. To using his power and being obeyed. To—using people.

In all sorts of ways…

Stop right there, she adjured herself fiercely.

Somehow she managed to keep her tone casual. 'Perhaps they don't like to flaunt their money in the current economic climate. That is—if it's true.'

'Of course it is,' said Millie. 'Kostas says they have homes in Athens and New York as well as this house. Eleni was born in New York, which is why she speaks such good English. She used to be Madame Constantinou's maid and she met Yorgos while the family were here on holiday. He didn't want to leave the island after they were married, so he became the major-domo here with Eleni as housekeeper. All nice and cosy. Although they have more to do since Alexis returned.'

She added more quietly, 'Kostas says he quarrelled with his father over his plans for Rhymnos. Or so everyone thinks.'

Selena's brows lifted. 'Kostas appears to be a mine of information,' she said drily.

Millie shrugged. 'I told you. The Constantinou family is a big deal on Rhymnos. However, I'm still getting married and I'll need my birth certificate. So don't forget.'

'I'll do my best,' Selena said drily. 'And I've remembered something else.' She delved into her pocket and produced the silver bracelet. 'I came across this on my travels.'

'I wondered where it had got to,' said Millie. She gave Selena a winning smile. 'The clasp's a bit dodgy so maybe you could get that fixed, too, and send it with the other stuff.'

She finished her coffee and stood up. 'Now, I'm going to change out of this foul dress and catch some rays by the pool.' As she turned to the door, it opened and Eleni came in with a tray and an apron which she handed to Millie.

Her voice was pleasant but firm. 'You will clear the table, if you please, *thespinis*, then bring the tray to the kitchen. Hara, our cook, will show you where everything is kept, and afterwards you will help her to begin preparations for the evening meal.'

Millie gasped. 'But we've just eaten,' she objected. 'And it's sweltering.'

'Even so, you will find that a tired and hungry man will require to be fed.' Eleni was inexorable. 'You must accustom yourself, Kyria Amelia.'

Selena braced herself for the hissy fit of the century. Instead Millie's shoulders slumped and she muttered a grudging acquiescence and began to pile the remaining china and cutlery on to the tray.

Selena cleared her throat. 'Can I do anything to help?'

'That would not be appropriate, *thespinis*.' The older woman spoke with chilly politeness. 'Not for a guest of Kyrios Alexis.' She beckoned to Millie. 'Come, little one.'

Well, that's me told, Selena thought without pleasure.

She hesitated for a moment, debating whether or not to go back to her room but decided it would be better not to treat it as her sole option, or it might soon seem like a prison cell.

Instead, she slid open the door to the courtyard, and emerged cautiously, feeling once again as if she was walking into a wall of heat.

During lunch, cushioned loungers and parasols had been arranged temptingly round the perimeter of the pool.

Selena dragged the nearest one into a patch of shade, adjusted its parasol to cover her completely, and lay down, aware within minutes that her pants and tunic were sticking to her sweat-dampened body.

She sent the pool a longing look, knowing at the same time it would make no difference when her bag arrived from the hotel, because her swimsuit was still in England.

I packed for a flying visit, she thought, not for sunbathing and swimming.

Just one of many reasons not to hang around but to go home and brave Aunt Nora's wrath.

The prime one being her need to avoid any further involvement with Alexis Constantinou.

Not that there's been much, she tried to tell herself. And certainly nothing serious. Especially on his part.

On the contrary, he'd merely been—amusing himself by playing with the senses of someone he'd instantly recognised as being totally inexperienced. Something of a novelty, no doubt, in the world he moved in.

Even something of a novelty in her own world, come to that.

But, for whatever reason—a belated sense of decency, or, more probably, a suspicion that her innocence might prove sexually unrewarding—he had not allowed those moments in the cave to proceed to their obvious conclusion.

Well, why would he, when he could probably have his pick from most of the women in the world?

And she should be grateful that he'd thought twice and go while the going was good.

Except there was still a chance—in fact, a distinct possibility—that Millie might start to have doubts, now that romance had truly collided with reality. Her expression in the dining room just now had indicated as much.

And if so, Selena told herself resolutely, I should stay to help tip the balance, maybe. I just hope she doesn't take too long to come to her senses.

While she ignored the sneaking suspicion she might just have taken leave of her own.

But as the days passed, Selena was forced to the conclusion that both her hopes and her fears were equally groundless.

To her surprise, Millie's sulks over the new regime had been relatively short-lived. She had accepted that she would only see Kostas on his afternoon off, and that part of their time together would be spent with Father Stephanos, so that she could learn about the Greek Orthodox religion.

Even more amazingly, she'd developed a penchant for cooking under the good-natured direction of Hara the cook, a large well-built lady who looked like a walking advertisement for her own skills.

In fact, the moussaka Millie had produced for lunch with something of a flourish the previous week had been delicious.

The plan, Selena thought grimly, was clearly not working. While her co-conspirator in all this seemed to have vanished off the radar.

Because, in nearly three weeks, Alexis Constantinou had not paid a single visit to the Villa Helios. Not a sight. Not a sound. Not even a message.

Not that she wanted him there, she hastened to assure herself, but although it had been a novelty at first to relax by the pool in the bikini airily proffered by Millie—'It belongs to Fiona. I must have packed it by mistake. Something else for you to take back when you go'—she was beginning to find it lonely, which was odd for someone so used to her own company, she thought wryly.

Also, even if she'd been interested in acquiring a tan, it was difficult to relax when each day increased her conviction that she was not truly welcome at the villa.

Eleni and Yorgos remained coolly polite and unswervingly formal while Penelope, whenever Selena tried to engage her in conversation, clearly could not wait to scuttle away.

She'd spent some of her time exploring her immediate surroundings, becoming familiar with the villa's layout around the central courtyard, while beyond the gardens at the rear and towards the broad headland, she'd found the landing area for the helicopter and the massive shed where it was kept.

But most of the time, she occupied herself with the small cache of British and American thrillers she'd found in a cupboard in the *saloni* and which, according to Eleni, had been left there by 'my lady, Madame Constantinou'. The information, accompanied by a heavy sigh, reminded Selena that Alexis had mentioned his parents were divorced.

Selena sighed, too, as she closed the current Elmore Leonard and prepared to go inside and change. Kostas was due soon, possibly accompanied by Father Stephanos, and Eleni had hinted heavily on the first occasion that it would be unbecoming to be seen in a bikini during these visits.

So, it was back to a cotton top and her button-through denim skirt, of which she was already heartily sick even though it was returned to her, like the rest of her meagre wardrobe, beautifully laundered after each wearing.

However, she just had enough time for another swim, she decided, walking to the pool and poising herself for her dive. This was the real luxury of the Villa Helios, she thought. Not the king-size bed, or the power shower, but this secluded expanse of turquoise water, the total opposite of the crowded public baths in Haylesford where it was almost impossible to swim even a few metres uninterrupted, and she would miss it when she left.

In fact, it was all that she would miss, she added with a touch of defiance, and dived in.

She powered one swift, invigorating length, relishing the coolness of the water against her warm skin then, as she turned, she took a deep breath and submerged completely, enjoying once more the sensation of being enclosed in a silent world ruled by the glow of the sun.

Only to become suddenly aware that a shadow had fallen across the brightness ahead of her, shifting with the ripples on the water as she got nearer.

Gasping, Selena surfaced, grabbing at the tiled rim with one hand and pushing her wet hair back from her face with the other as she looked up. And found Alexis, waiting silently. Looking down.

Something—an amalgam of joy and fear—lurched inside her. Joy at seeing him again at last. Fear of revealing too much of the thoughts and dreams that had haunted her waking and sleeping since he'd walked away from her at the hotel.

The unguessed at longings, potent and unforgettable, that he'd awoken in a few short moments. And as quickly regretted. That, she knew, was what she should remember, just as much as she needed to hide the rest.

He said, 'Did I startle you, Selene *mou*?'

She hunched a shoulder. Tried for nonchalance. 'A little. I didn't know you were expected.'

'I was not.' He added softly, 'And I did not expect to disturb a water nymph.'

'Oh' seemed the only, if inadequate, answer to that. She felt silly, there in the water, gaping up at him like a goldfish in a bowl, but as she went to haul herself out of the pool, he reached down, his hands firm under her armpits, and lifted her bodily, and all too easily, on to the tiles.

In the next instant, he'd unslung the towel—her towel—draped across his shoulder, and wrapped it round her, tucking in the edge above her breasts to secure it.

The contact with her skin was infinitesimal, but it ran like wildfire through every pore—every nerve-ending.

'I think,' he said quietly, his dark gaze holding hers endlessly, almost mesmerisingly, 'that we need to talk.'

'Yes—perhaps so. I—I'll just go and get dressed…'

'And I will wait here.' His hands descended on her tense shoulders, directing her towards her room.

She showered, then rough-dried her hair, dropping the brush twice, her fingers all thumbs, knowing—and resenting that she was unnerved by Alexis's sudden re-appearance.

We'll talk and he'll go, she told herself. That's all there is to it, so calm down.

She opened the wardrobe and reached for the shelf where her clean underwear was deposited each day. But although her lace-trimmed briefs were there in a neat pile, there was no sign of her bra. Oh, hell, she muttered under her breath. It must have been taken to Millie's room again.

And she didn't have time to hunt through that particular chaos.

She picked a white vest top in ribbed cotton, which, she decided, was sufficiently concealing, then buttoned on her denim skirt, and went out into the courtyard to join him.

She said flatly, 'Obviously, we need to discuss Millie and what to do next, because Plan A has failed and we don't have a Plan B.'

She paused. 'Did you know that a couple of days ago, she actually made a feta cheese? *A feta cheese.* For Kostas to take to his mother.' She sighed. 'You have to admit she's been clever.'

'Determined, certainly.' His tone was dry. 'But Anna Papoulis is equally so, and her mind is fixed on a substantial dowry for her handsome boy.' He paused.

'Perhaps if your aunt will give her nothing, she might be persuaded to come here and say so. It could lead to the result she desires.'

He added brusquely, 'Her leg must have healed by now.'

Selena hesitated. 'It's out of plaster, but apparently she's having serious physiotherapy every day. And her mind is made up. Millie goes home. No compromise.'

His brows lifted. 'So, you have spoken to her?'

'Only briefly. She's either having treatment or she's out.' Selena shrugged. 'Her friends are gathering round, taking her for little trips in their cars to provide her with a change of scene.'

'She would not regard Rhymnos as a change of scene?' Alexis asked ironically.

'No,' Selena said baldly. 'As a climb-down.'

She looked down at the ground. 'You really think

that Millie having no money could be a deal-breaker and Kostas's mother will force him to give her up?'

'She will try,' he said drily. 'But perhaps she will discover that love is not so easily dismissed from the heart and the mind.'

'Then you believe Kostas really does care about Millie?'

Alexis shrugged. 'He shows every sign of it. In my bar now, he sells only drinks, not his—company.'

Selena flushed. 'Well, that's a good choice,' she returned awkwardly.

'He is fortunate he can make it.' There was an odd harshness in his voice, and she looked up at him, startled.

His smile was reassuring. 'But on this lovely day, I, too, have choices and I choose to show you Rhymnos—if you will come with me.' He added wryly, 'Your aunt should not be the only one to have a change of scene.'

She knew she should not do this. That she should invent an excuse—any excuse. But she could hardly claim to be busy when he'd found her in the pool.

And maybe she could risk one day in his company before she finally admitted defeat and went home. Or what passed for home anyway, she thought wryly, imagining the atmosphere that her failure would engender.

Although she didn't have to stay in Haylesford, she reminded herself. Millie's future was no longer a consideration, and she could get on with her own life.

If she could find another job before the next term began, she could even begin to establish her future independence right away.

He said, 'Well, say something, Selena *mou*.' His tone was faintly mocking as if he was expecting her to refuse his offer. 'Just tell me if you wish to be left in peace.'

Peace. The word stung at her brain, sending her into renewed turmoil.

*What peace is there in never seeing you again?* she wanted to cry. When I know that, in spite of myself, you've been there in my head every day and every night since I arrived on this island.

Do I really need to deprive myself of a final hour or two in his company—knowing how precious their memory will be? Or to let him know I'm scared to be alone with him?

She met his quizzical gaze with sudden recklessness, her mouth relaxing into a smile. 'I should like to see more of Rhymnos—before I leave.' Adding, *'Efharisto.'*

*'Parakalo,'* he returned and smiled back at her. 'So—shall we go?'

And that, she thought, was how, swiftly and easily, she'd made the choice which had changed her life for ever.

# CHAPTER SEVEN

It HADN'T SEEMED like that at the time, of course.

He was just being a good host, she'd told herself, but that hadn't stopped her wanting to dance at his side as they made their way out of the courtyard. And not even glimpsing Eleni frowning at the *saloni* window could spoil her mood.

So where could they be going? she wondered as he started the Jeep. After all, there couldn't be much of the island that hadn't been already covered during their search for Millie and Kostas.

Unless he was planning to take her back to the cave...

Even the thought of it was enough to send her body tingling into dangerous warmth, shocking her with the force of her own yearning.

To hide her confusion, she hurried into speech. 'This is very good of you.'

'Not at all.' He paused. 'I thought you might like to discover a little more about our most important industry.'

*Geography and economics...*

Disappointment was almost choking her but she kept

her tone bright. 'Am I going to see round Rhymnos Oil? How marvellous.'

'Not now,' he said. 'Not today.' He turned the Jeep to the right, following the rough road along the coast, between the sea and yet more olive groves, all new territory for her. 'Instead, we shall go back to where it all began.'

*With some history thrown in...*

Her mouth was beginning to ache with the effort of smiling, but she persevered. He was being kind and she needed to be grateful. Which was all he would expect from her in return.

But already, she was far too conscious of his presence beside her. Much too aware of his dark sculpted profile and the movement of his lean, strong hands on the wheel of the Jeep, evoking memories of his touch it was far safer to forget.

She forced herself to turn her head and concentrate on the sea, the faint breeze barely troubling its azure smoothness today as it stretched out to the horizon and beyond. A distance that, very soon, she would be covering on her journey back to England.

The prospect of her return and its inevitable confrontation with Aunt Nora was not one she relished.

She would be thankful when term recommenced and she could lose herself in the demands of her course work, she thought, feeling her eyes sting and telling herself it was just the dazzle of the sun on the water.

'What troubles you, Selene *mou*?'

His question jolted her. She hadn't realised she was being observed in her turn and she looked back at him, flushing a little. 'Oh, the usual back-to-reality blues, I guess.'

'Rhymnos has not seemed real to you?'

No, she thought, as longing tightened her throat. Because of you, it's turned into a wild, impossible dream. And I don't want to wake...

By some superhuman effort, she shrugged. Kept her tone casual. 'Well, hardly—under the circumstances. If I'd come here on my own account, it might have been different.'

'Ah,' he said softly. 'Then do you think you will come back?'

*If you asked me, I'd stay...*

And where had that come from? she asked herself wretchedly, nailing on another smile and thanking heaven she hadn't spoken aloud. 'Oh, one day, perhaps, in the distant future when I'm no longer a struggling student but qualified and working. Who knows?'

'Who, indeed, *agapi mou.*' There was an odd note in his voice. 'So we must make the most of what time we have left.'

Sudden anger flared inside her. She wanted to turn on him. To demand, 'If you think that—if you *really* think that, then why have you stayed away all this time? Why have you left me alone to wonder—and suffer through these empty days? And what's this afternoon all about? Crumbs from the rich man's table?'

But she bit back the words, because these were dangerous questions which, in all honesty, she had no right to ask. And, probably, would receive answers she didn't want to hear.

Leave it there, she adjured herself. Accept what there is. Hope for nothing more.

She realised that Alexis was turning the Jeep inland up a well-worn track through the shade of yet another massive olive grove, their route flanked by trees with trunks so gnarled and twisted they looked a thousand years old. And perhaps they were long past their 'best by' date because for the life of her, even by craning her neck, she could see no sign of any fruit.

Eventually, she broke the silence. 'Are these your trees? I suppose you must be thinking of replacing them.'

He shot her a swift, amused glance. 'Yes, they are mine and, on the contrary, Selene *mou*, I am expecting them to bring me a wonderful harvest in November.'

'Truly?' She gave the overhanging branches another dubious look.

'The olives are still tiny,' he said. 'But they are there.'

She was half expecting him to stop the Jeep and show her, but he drove on, accelerating up the slight slope which, eventually, rose more steeply as it took them out of the shelter of the grove towards the grassy upland beyond.

Where he stopped, parking the Jeep under another massive tree, its leaves shimmering in the sunlight.

He reached into the back of the Jeep and extracted a rucksack. He said, 'From here we walk, Selene *mou*.'

'Oh.' She swallowed, glancing at the rock-crowned hills ahead of them. 'I'm not really dressed for mountaineering.'

He slanted a smile at her. 'You need not fear. It is not far and we go round, not up.'

The tussocky grass, studded with wildflowers, was springy under her feet, and Alexis reached for her hand and steadied her as they walked, skirting the steeper slopes as they headed round the curve of the hill.

And there cradled in its folds as if set down there by some giant hand were three tall pillars of creamy stone rearing towards the sky from their flat rocky platform, all of it encircled by grass, green as an emerald.

Instantly, prosaically familiar from bottles on a supermarket shelf and yet, in their proper setting, startling and somehow alien, part of an entirely different world, ancient and mysterious.

Alexis said softly, 'The pillars of Apollo, *agapi mou*. All that still remains of his temple. My own private sanctuary since I was a young boy. Where I have always come to think about what I truly wanted from my life. And the place where Rhymnos Oil became for me more than just a dream.'

She took a deep breath. 'It's—beautiful.' She hesitated. 'But it can't always have been private. Not with holidaymakers swarming all over it.'

He shook his head. 'They come to Rhymnos for the beaches and *tavernas*. There's nothing here to tempt them. It is not Delphi. There's no cave for an oracle or glorious statuary waiting to be uncovered like buried treasure. It is just another small ruin.'

She said quietly, her heartbeat quickening, 'But special to you.'

'Yes. For so many reasons.' He paused, looking at her, his gaze broodingly intense as it held hers. 'Shall we go down?'

The slope of the ground was gentle but Selena felt as if she was standing on the edge of an abyss. That one false move and she would fall quietly—endlessly into oblivion.

You don't need to be here, whispered the voice in her head. You already know what you're doing with your life. You can't risk any second thoughts—especially when they're foolish and impossible.

But you can always step back. Take your hand from his. Make an excuse. Tell him you're leaving early tomorrow and you need to pack. Tell him something. Anything that will get you back to safety.

Only to hear herself say haltingly, 'Yes, that would be good.'

Silence folded round them as they walked down to the temple. Not the hush she'd sensed on that other day before the storm, but something deeper and even more intimate than the clasp of his fingers round hers. And infinitely more dangerous.

At the foot of the slope, the ground levelled out, its cover of grass even as a carpet, soft and springy underfoot.

Alexis released her hand and she moved forward, climbing up the two steps which led to the rocky floor of the shrine, and looking across to the tumble of fallen masonry below the columns, which, she supposed, must once have been an altar.

How many thousands of years ago, she wondered, had people built this place and come there with their offerings?

A breeze like a sigh moved between the columns,

bringing with it a delicate almost spicy scent. Oregano, she thought wonderingly as she breathed it, mint and thyme. Did they grow wild here?

She turned to ask Alexis and saw that he'd taken a rug from his rucksack and spread it in the shade of two large rectangular stones and was now reclining, very much at his ease, drinking from a bottle of water.

He produced another, uncapped it and held it out to her. 'Are you thirsty after our walk?'

It made no sense to deny it. She walked back slowly and took the bottle from him, taking care to sit on the furthest edge of the rug.

How quiet it was, she thought, letting the water trickle blissfully down her throat. And—how remote. Too remote and too quiet.

And she needed to leave, she told herself with sudden unease, while she still could.

Find some excuse to cut the afternoon short and go back to the house. But what could she say? That her sister would be worried, when he must know as well as she did that Millie never gave her a second thought?

But she could at least break this dangerous silence.

She rushed into speech. 'Why Apollo? I thought Zeus was the most important Greek god.'

He smiled. 'On Rhymnos, it was always Apollo. Eleni's mother, who was my nurse when I was a baby, was born here, too, and she filled my head with all the old legends. How he was Apollo the Healer, the god of music and poetry as well as prophecy. How as Phoebus Apollo he drove the chariot of the sun across the sky each day.'

'Wow.' This was better. This was casual conversation, she thought as she smiled back. 'A god of many talents. And I thought all he did was chase girls.'

'He found time for that, too,' Alexis agreed solemnly. 'Or he would have had no sons.'

'And that was important—even for a god?'

'I think—for anyone,' he said, after a pause. 'Besides one of his sons, Asclepius, became the father of medicine and another, Aristaeus, taught the Greeks agriculture. How to keep bees, to look after livestock, to grow olives, and even make cheese.' He added lightly, 'So we should be thankful.'

She matched his tone. 'While I know who's really responsible for Millie's sudden expertise in the kitchen.'

'*Efharisto,*' he said. 'I thought you would blame me.'

'Hardly.' She sighed. 'She seems determined to prove herself, but I still feel it's far too soon for her to commit herself like this.'

'Ah,' he said softly. 'So you do not believe that sometimes all that it takes is a look—a word—in order to be lost for ever?'

Selena swallowed. 'No, I don't,' she said defiantly.

Adding silently, *I can't—I won't believe it. I need it to be impossible. Need it so very badly...*

'Tell me something, Selene *mou.*' His tone was almost idle. 'How many times have you telephoned to England since you came to my house?'

She gave him a wary look. 'I suppose—about six. And I intend to pay for my calls before I leave,' she added defensively.

'That will not be necessary.' His tone permitted no

argument. 'But all these calls, I think, have been to your aunt's house. None of them to your man.'

Damnation, she thought, biting her lip. Why had she ever thought it was a good idea to invent him?

She said stiffly, 'I think that's my business.'

'Even so, how will he regard so long a silence?'

She lifted her chin. 'He'll understand.'

'Understand?' Alexis repeated incredulously. 'In his shoes, I would have been here before a week had passed, searching the island for you.'

'I told you—he's busy.'

'So busy that he can forget the smoothness of your skin, the scent of your hair, the sweetness of your mouth?'

She gasped, feeling a rush of hot colour suffuse her face.

'You—you have no right to say such things,' she accused breathlessly.

'I have every right.' He spoke with quiet intensity as he took the bottle from her hand, replacing its cap and setting it to one side. 'Because I, may God help me, have forgotten nothing. And I never can.'

Her mind was suddenly in freefall. He did not seem to have moved, yet the space between them had somehow dwindled to nothing.

And, equally somehow, he'd recaptured her hand, brushing its palm gently with his lips, his teeth grazing the soft mound at the base of her thumb, sending little tremors shimmering through her nerve endings.

She closed her eyes, shutting out the image of his dark head bent so near her own.

She thought, *Oh, God, I have to stop this. Now...*

But the heavy beat of the sun against her eyelids was already echoing in the thud of her pulses, as if telling her over and over again 'too late—too late.'

And then he was raising her hand, placing it on his shoulder and she could quite easily have snatched it back, but instead found her fingers tracing bone and muscle, then curling into the warmth of his skin beneath the crisp cotton shirt as his arms went round her drawing her to him.

His hands slipped under her top, and as he stroked her bare back, following the path of her spine up to the delicate wings of her shoulder blades, she found her body involuntarily arching towards him, her lips parting in a tiny gasp of remembered delight at his touch.

In the next instant, his mouth sought and took hers, probing its inner sweetness, teasing her with the glide of his tongue against hers, while his hands slid deftly round her body, cupping her untrammelled breasts, strumming her hardening nipples with his thumbs until they burned and ached with a pleasure that was almost pain.

She moaned softly into his mouth, melting into his kiss, sharing its ardour, answering its demand and basking in its moisture as her tongue tangled with his in enthralled exploration. Her body was straining against his as if seeking to be absorbed into its heat—its strength. Her reeling mind, dismissing the shyness and reticence that until then had been her safeguard, was telling her that this was what she'd been born for.

This hour. This place. This man.

When at last he raised his head, his dark eyes looked blurred, almost dazed. He said unsteadily, his voice hoarse with yearning, 'Do you know how lovely you are, Selene *mou*? How badly I need to look at you—to know how beautiful you truly are.'

She stared back at him, her eyes widening as she realised what he was asking. And, for a moment, she was assailed by doubt, wondering how she would endure it if the next time their eyes met, she saw disappointment.

*'Se thelo poli, agapi mou.'* His words were a whispered caress, turning any remaining fear to hunger. 'I want you so very much, my darling. Let me know that you want me, too.'

Selena sat up slowly. She put her hand against his face, running her fingers along his cheekbone then down to the strong line of his jaw, savouring the faint roughness of his skin.

Taking a deep breath, she pulled her vest top over her head and tossed it aside, then lay back on the rug, smiling up at him.

She saw a muscle move in his taut throat, then he bent to her, taking one rounded breast and then the other in his lips and suckling them gently, his tongue flicking the tumescent nipples with sensuous precision.

And she heard herself cry out huskily in a voice she hardly recognised. A voice that expressed a longing as deep and as urgent as his own.

'Yes,' he said. 'Yes, *matia mou*. I promise.'

He began to unbutton her skirt, beginning at its hem, then moving slowly, even carefully, up to the waist band, before peeling the edges apart, as if unveiling some infinitely precious work of art, leaving her with only a last few inches of lace-trimmed fabric to cover her.

Letting her see the glow in his gaze, and the tenderness and pleasure that curved his firm mouth as he studied her.

As he started to touch her again.

His fingers were almost miraculously gentle, feathering across her shoulders and stroking the soft underside of her arms before returning to her breasts, his lips following the path of his hands over every curve and hollow. Moving downwards with tantalising languor, smoothing the flatness of her stomach, and toying with the inner whorls of her navel. Outlining the graceful jut of her hip bones, then sliding a hand under the rim of her briefs and easing them off, stripping her deftly and completely.

She heard him draw a deep sighing breath as he looked down at her, his hands gliding the length of her body from throat to instep, and then back to her slender thighs, stroking them, coaxing them apart as if he knew that the soft trembling of her flesh was prompted as much by shyness as excitement.

'Trust me, *agapi mou*.' The whispered words were raw. 'Let me learn to please you a little.'

His hand moved, exploring the delicate folds of her womanhood to find the tiny aching mound they concealed and caress it slowly with his fingertips.

His touch still gentle, but also wickedly sure. Banishing any lingering doubts and leading her instead to acceptance. And, unhurriedly, to the sensual tumult of physical arousal.

The time for resistance, if it had ever been a possibility, was long gone.

Selena lay, eyes half-closed in surrender, every thought, every nerve ending concentrated almost painfully on her body's astonished response to every new, delicious sensation.

Hearing the tiny moan she was unable to control as his subtle, all too knowing fingers pushed lightly into the silken, soaking heat of her, pausing, waiting, perhaps for some sign of discomfort, before penetrating her more deeply. Offering her a sweetly piercing foretaste of her future initiation.

She moved restlessly against the thrust of his fingers, instinct telling her that she wanted the future to become the present. That she needed to feel his skin naked against hers. To know the stark male hardness of him sheathed inside her and possess him in turn. And found herself reaching for him, fumbling with the fastening at the waistband of his chinos.

'Ah, no, *matia mou*.' His voice ragged, Alexis captured her wrists, placing her hands at her sides. Holding them there. 'This is for you, my sweet one. Only for you.'

And bent to her again. Only, this time, using his mouth, his tongue brushing like gossamer against her burning tumescent urgency. Circling it, flickering on it fiercely—exquisitely.

Making her writhe and quiver in helpless almost shocked abandonment at this ultimate intimacy, and, at the same time, becoming aware of some strange knot of tension tightening deeply, inexorably inside her, taking her to the very edge of endurance.

Her voice pleading, breaking, she cried out something that might have been his name, then the knot snapped and she was free, flung wildly into a tumbling, throbbing chaos where the sharp, sweet, clenching spasms of pleasure were hardly distinguishable from pain.

Held there, then slowly released, the tremors dying away leaving her body and its senses calmed and at peace as she floated back to the reality of Alexis's arms holding her close and his voice murmuring softly, tenderly in his own language. Plus the additional discovery that she was looking at him through a blur of tears.

Shaken by all kinds of embarrassment, Selena sat up, scrubbing at her eyes like a child while she tried desperately to think how to react, silently cursing the lack of sophistication that might have carried her through this awkwardness. And eventually decided only the truth would do.

She swallowed. 'I—I don't know what to say.'

He said quietly, almost ruefully, 'I think I, too, am a little lost for words, Selene *mou*.'

She bit her lip. 'However, I think I should get dressed—unless you…' She stumbled a little. 'Unless, of course, you want…'

He reached for her clothes and handed them to her.

'As I told you, *agapi mou*. This was for you alone.' He smiled at her, adding softly, 'I can wait.'

He got to his feet and walked away towards the temple, waiting, his back turned, while Selena huddled on her garments. For which, she realised, she was grateful. Absurdly so in view of what he had just seen and done. But now, in the aftermath, she felt distinctly self-conscious. And uncertain. Also uncomfortable as her clothing seemed to rasp against her still sensitised skin.

At last, she said, 'I'm ready.' And when he remained where he was, staring silently ahead of him, she repeated the words more loudly.

He turned back instantly, smiling again but this time with an obvious effort. 'My apologies, Selene *mou*.

'Once again, I was thinking.'

Thinking, she wondered, or regretting?

And this question continued to occupy her own thoughts all the way back to the villa.

# CHAPTER EIGHT

SHE MUST, SELENA THOUGHT, have taken leave of her
senses. Although it might be fairer to say she'd been
robbed of them. Or seduced out of them.

Except, her common sense told her it had not been a
conventional seduction by any means. In fact, she wasn't
really sure how to describe it—or justify the long, sweet
shiver that ran through her as she remembered.

But what should she make of the subsequent silent
journey back to the villa?

Thankfully, she was alone. Millie, absorbed in Kostas, probably hadn't noticed her absence, so she had
time to recover her equilibrium and come to terms with
what had happened.

Because, very soon, she would have to face Alexis
again at dinner, without blushing, stammering or falling over her feet.

And it seemed important that when they met, she
should not be wearing the clothes he had so recently
removed with such lingering skill.

Do not, she adjured herself, pressing her hands to her
burning cheeks, even go there. Stay sane.

A change of clothing didn't offer much choice. The blue tunic also held memories best forgotten. So she decided on her Capri pants and the nondescript white shirt, bought in her final school year.

Also, she needed to do something with her hair. Leaving it loose would only remind her of his fingers twining it as he kissed her, and plaiting seemed too obvious, so she simply scooped it back, securing it at the nape of her neck with an elastic band.

But her precautions, if that's what they were, proved unnecessary because Alexis was not at dinner, having returned to the hotel, according to Millie, taking Kostas with him.

Selena ate her meal on autopilot, her mind veering between blankness and bewilderment.

It seemed, after all, that he'd just—walked away. That he'd just been playing some unkind game with her senses. Amusing himself by breaking down the inhibitions of this little English virgin who'd come blundering into his life.

And who would waste no time about blundering right out again, she told herself, her throat tightening.

'For God's sake, Lena,' Millie said impatiently. 'Are you deaf or in a trance? I've asked you twice when you're going back to England because I really need my birth certificate.'

'Would tomorrow suit you?'

'Well—fine.' Millie gave her a surprised look. 'I really hope Aunt Nora doesn't give you a hard time,' she offered awkwardly.

Selena shrugged. 'I expect by now she's accepted the situation. Shall I send the paperwork here?'

'No, to Kostas at the hotel.' Millie paused. 'I'm leaving, too, going to stay with his Aunt Evanthia, who lives just outside town.'

Selena's brows rose. 'His mother's sister?' she enquired dubiously.

'His father's. Chalk and cheese, apparently.' Millie gave a slight giggle. 'It'll be more convenient, and besides, I guess we've both overstayed our welcome here, don't you?'

In my case, from the moment I got here, thought Selena. She said quietly, 'Probably.'

She was packing her bag when Eleni came in with a small pile of clean laundry.

Selena looked across the bed at her. 'I'm returning home tomorrow, Kyria Validis. Will your husband be able to drive me to the ferry?'

She saw a flash of surprise in Eleni's eyes and what she'd have sworn was relief but the housekeeper's voice held only its usual unemotional civility.

'Of course, *thespinis*. You wish to take the morning boat, perhaps? Shall I tell Yorgos ten a.m.?'

'That would be perfect,' Selena returned equally levelly.

At the door Eleni hesitated as if she was about to say something else, then turned and left in silence.

Selena sighed and added the clean clothes to her bag, switching her thoughts determinedly to her travel plans. She wasn't sure how soon she could get a flight from Mykonos, but there was enough credit on the cash card

Aunt Nora had grudgingly supplied to tide her over for a night or two.

But any uncertainty would be worth it if it rescued her from the present situation.

If, she thought, it saves me from myself. From this stranger I never knew existed, but who's living in my head. In my body...

But then she'd never been seriously attracted to anyone before. She'd always been too busy—or too shy.

Until now...

She bit down hard on her lip, tormented by the memory of how swiftly and eagerly she'd surrendered.

As if her life had been spent waiting for this moment. This man.

Delusional, she thought. Pathetic.

And how long would it take to get over this ridiculous weakness? To forget Alexis with the same ease that he had demonstrated over her—leaving without a word?

When term starts, it will be easier, she told herself. Until then I'll get a job—waiting on tables, stacking shelves—anything to keep me occupied.

And soon these weeks in Greece will seem like a bad dream.

If she'd thought an early night would relax her, she soon discovered she was wrong. At last, around midnight, she finally fell into a restless doze, only to find herself suddenly sitting bolt upright, staring into the darkness, her heart hammering.

The room felt airless and oppressive, so maybe this was why she couldn't sleep properly, yet it seemed churlish to complain of the heat when before long she'd be faced with an English winter.

However, it might be worth risking a stray mosquito by pushing back the shutters in search of a night breeze from the pool.

Her nightdress clinging to her, she slid off the crumpled bed, pushing back her hair from her damp forehead and relishing the coolness of the floor against her bare feet.

The shutters glided noiselessly open and she stepped through into the courtyard, and halted abruptly, aware that she wasn't alone. That someone who'd been stretched out on one of the loungers in front of her was rising to his feet.

And not just someone, she realised incredulously as Alexis said softly, 'So there you are.'

She found her voice. 'What are you doing here?'

'Waiting,' he said. 'Again. For you.'

'You went back to the hotel.'

'I had some business to complete.' He was watching her, barefoot like herself and tightening the belt of his towelling robe. 'It is done, so I returned.'

'Yes—but...' She hesitated nervously.

'But?' he queried.

Selena spread her hands almost helplessly. 'You said you were waiting but you couldn't possibly know that I'd still be awake, let alone that I'd come out here.'

He shrugged. 'I was unable to sleep. I thought you might have the same difficulty.' He took a step towards her. 'And for the same reason.'

'I—I don't know what you mean.'

He clicked his tongue reprovingly. 'That is unworthy of you, *agapi mou*. Also untrue.'

'I—I'm just concerned about the journey,' she improvised swiftly, almost desperately. 'You see, I'm leaving tomorrow. Going home.'

He walked to her. He said huskily, 'Then it is as well we have the rest of the night.' And lifting her into his arms, he carried her down the courtyard to a room at the end where a shaded lamp burned dimly beside the bed.

His room, Selena thought dazedly. His bed. Also waiting...

And she needed to say something—do something to stop this here and now before the afternoon's mistake turned into the night's disaster.

Instead, she found herself turning her face into his shoulder, her resolution faltering as she breathed the scent of his skin, her body curving ever more closely to the warmth and strength of his own.

Just this once, she begged whatever gods were listening. Let me have this one memory and then I'll go far away. Back to my old life, but able to deal with it in a better way.

And she slid her arm round his neck, pulling him down to her waiting lips. His kiss was tender but beneath the gentleness, she already sensed a new dark urgency—a force as yet unleashed, and found herself suddenly hesitant.

Alexis lifted his head, looking down into her widening eyes. 'You must not be afraid, *matia mou*,' he murmured as he put her down on the bed. 'Not of me.

Never of me. How can I hurt my own soul?' He smiled at her, stroking the curve of her face then walked over to fasten the shutters and draw the filmy curtains, closing them in together before taking off his robe.

Beneath it, he was naked. And, although she had no grounds for comparison, magnificently so, she realised, any initial shyness or apprehension dissolving, and her gaze absorbed, even hungry as he came back to the bed. And to her.

'Don't look at me like that, *agapi mou*.' There was laughter in his voice as he stretched out beside her. 'You will embarrass me.'

'How do I look?' she whispered, smiling as he drew her into his arms.

'Like a little cat,' he said softly. 'With a saucer of cream.'

And he began to kiss her again, his mouth caressing hers, then skimming her forehead, her eyes, her cheekbones and slowly back to her parted, eager lips.

He slid the straps of her nightgown from her shoulders and eased it down her body until she was completely free from its thin folds.

He said softly, 'I have dreamed of you like this, *agapi mou*, naked in my bed, your hair like moonlight on my pillow. And now my dream has come true.'

He tossed her nightgown to the floor and began to stroke her breasts, her nipples rising and hardening under the skilful play of his fingers, drawing a sigh of pleasure from her, which turned to a husky moan as his lips took each dusky peak in turn and suckled them slowly and sweetly.

'Exquisite,' he whispered against her skin. 'Like perfect roses, Selene *mou*.'

Then once again, his mouth found hers, capturing its soft contours, his tongue moving like silk against her own, and Selena wound her arms round his neck, playing with the thick hair that grew at its nape, surrendering to the implicit promise of his kiss.

His hands slid down her back, tracing the pliant length of her spine and moulding the slight curves of her buttocks, as he gathered her closer, so that the proud strength of his penis pressed against her belly, and she felt the hot rush of moisture between her thighs that signalled her body's readiness to welcome him.

She moved beneath him, her body seething, restless, her hands exploring him in turn, closing round him, cupping him with unashamed greed.

'Please.' She hardly recognised her own voice. 'Oh—please.'

'Soon,' he whispered hoarsely. 'Have patience, my sweet one. First, let me protect you.'

He lifted himself away, reaching into a drawer in the night table, extracting and tearing open a small packet.

Safe sex, she thought from some still rational corner of her brain. That was what he meant, of course. But there could be no such thing. Even from her limited and incomplete experience she knew that. Because sex was wild—exciting—dangerous—taking your mind and your body by storm. Never *safe*...

Then he came back to her, and she stopped thinking as his hand reclaimed her, his fingertips parting the delicate petals of her womanhood to find the liquid heat they sheltered.

She arched towards him, gasping as, once again, he stroked her swollen crest, awakening it to aching delicious torment. Urging her towards release, then holding back, making her wait, prolonging her anticipation of the exquisite moment.

Her mouth searched for his, kissing him feverishly, almost desperately, sobbing soundlessly, her teeth grazing his bottom lip.

He said her name softly and fiercely. Then his hand moved with intense precision and took her at last over the edge, her body convulsing harshly as she was lifted to the peak of rapture.

She cried out, brokenly, blind-eyed with joy, and, in the same moment, was aware of him raising himself, moving across her, his arms braced on either side of her, before entering her still throbbing body with one powerful, fluid thrust.

For an instant, he paused, his gaze intent, even questioning, as if searching hers for a hint of reluctance or discomfort. Then, gently, unhurriedly, he began to push more deeply into her, making her want more.

So much more. Making her realise it was all there—waiting for her.

Telling her to reach for him. To grasp his shoulders. To lift her legs so that they locked round his lean hips. To move with him—against him—in this unique rhythm. To feel herself closing round the strong heated hardness of him, her muscles holding him. Taking all of him in this driving compulsion to be one with him.

At once, the pace of their joining quickened.

Intensified. She was caught, carried along by the fierce current of their mutual desire, every atom of her being concentrated on the sensations that seemed to be once more gathering inside her, drawing her, incredibly—inexorably—on a renewed ascent to pleasure.

No, she thought dazedly. Impossible so soon…

Yet, at that moment, it was there. She was seized and flung out, gasping, trembling and crying out wordlessly into the stormy tumult of climax, and, at its height, she heard Alexis groan harshly and felt his body shudder into hers in his own fierce release.

They lay still entwined together as their ragged breathing steadied and a kind of peace returned. At last, Alexis withdrew from her gently and went to the bathroom.

When he came back to the bed, he pulled her into his arms, cushioning her head on his chest, pushing her sweat-dampened hair back from her forehead.

'So, my heart's angel,' he whispered. 'Have you nothing to say?'

She gave a lingering sigh. 'It was—unbelievable.'

'I am sorry you think so.' There was laughter in his voice. 'I shall try to be more convincing next time.'

She giggled softly. 'And when will that be, Kyrios Alexis?'

'When I have recovered a little,' he returned, kissing the top of her head. 'It was only the gods who were made all-potent and untiring when they made love, *agapi mou*. Sadly, they denied mortal men the same gifts, and gave them only to women.'

She snuggled closer. 'How very unkind of them.'

'I have always believed so. But I thought, while we waited, you might like to learn a little Greek.'

'Why not?' She traced a pattern among his chest hair with her forefinger. 'What do you want me to say?'

'Let us begin with—*s'agapo.*'

'*S'agapo,*' she repeated obediently. 'What does that mean?'

'It means,' he said softly, 'that you have told me you love me.'

She gave an indignant gasp. 'Oh—but that's…'

He silenced her with a kiss. 'Is it untrue? Do you still claim that love cannot happen so quickly or so completely?'

She was silent for a moment, then she said huskily, 'Yesterday, I'd have said yes. Now—I just don't know any more. And it's not just about—this. It's when you take my hand and I—I feel suddenly—safe. As if…' She hesitated.

'As if you have come home?' Alexis supplied gently.

'Because that is how it is for me, *matia mou.*'

'Then why did you—vanish like that? Leave me out in the cold again?' She stopped abruptly. 'Oh, God, that sounds awful—so *needy.*'

'But I also have needs, Selene *mou.* And a question for you to ask me. *M'agapas?* Do you love me?'

She said quickly, painfully, 'Alexis—you don't have to…'

Only to be halted by another kiss.

'Ask me,' he whispered.

She lifted a hand. Touched his cheek. '*M'agapas*, Alexis *mou*?'

He took her hand. Held it. He said quietly, 'Yes, my beautiful one. I think almost from that first moment. And I shall love you for the rest of my life.'

He paused. 'But, I will confess I did not bargain for it. Maybe I felt there was no place for it in my life, and that is why I distanced myself.'

His mouth twisted. 'Only to discover that there was not an hour in every day that I did not think of you. When I did not long to be with you, to see that little jerk of the chin you give when you are about to cut me down to size.

'Or when I did not remember how you felt in my arms and the sweetness of your mouth.

'But when I came back, you told me you were leaving.' He drew a deep breath. 'That must not be, *agapi mou*. Not now. We cannot return to the cold when we belong together.'

Selena bit her lip. 'But I must go back. Millie needs her birth certificate and…'

'There is time for that. Time that we need together.' He spoke firmly. 'Stay with me here, *matia mou*, until I am free to travel to England with you.'

She stared at him. 'But my aunt…'

'I shall face her with you,' he said. 'When that time comes.'

Her little laugh was breathless. 'You must really love me.'

'Believe it.' He sounded almost fierce. 'Believe it always.'

He framed her face in his hands, brought her mouth to his, the kiss deep, lingering and warmly sensuous, leaving her sighing with pleasure.

She ran her fingers over his chest, stroking the flat male nipples, tracing the strength of his ribcage, enjoying the quickening of his heartbeat at her touch.

Emboldened, she let her hand drift down across his abdomen to rest on his hip and then slip further, feeling him stir and harden as her fingers clasped him. Caressed him.

Alexis sank back against the pillows, eyes half-closed and a faint smile playing about his mouth.

He said very softly, 'What are you doing, Selene *mou*?'

'Being a little cat,' she whispered back. 'Waiting for my next saucer of cream.'

She woke to the dazzle of sunlight and Millie's voice saying, 'Wake up, Lena, for heaven's sake. You've got a ferry to catch.'

Selena shot bolt upright, gasping, to the realisation that she was not only back in her own room, but once more chastely clad in her nightdress.

As if, in fact, the previous night had never happened.

But the slight aches she was experiencing, plus the feeling of languid well-being suffusing her told a different story.

Alexis, she thought, must have carried her back here and put her to bed like a little girl. And she suppressed a giggle.

Millie handed her a cup of coffee. 'It's all been kicking off here,' she said. 'Eleni and her beloved Kyrios

Alexis, the one who can do no wrong, having the mother and father of all rows.'

Selena's hand jerked, nearly spilling the coffee. 'Do you know what it was about?' She tried to sound casual.

Millie shrugged. 'How could I? I don't speak Greek. But I expect I can find out from Kostas,' she added. 'He knows everything that goes on.'

She paused. 'Don't forget about my bracelet, and you'd better return Fiona's bikini to her, if she still wants it.

'And please do your best to mend fences for me with Aunt Nora. Get her to come to the wedding. Apparently on Rhymnos, they know how to throw quite a party.'

She left Selena feeling dazed and uneasy. And when, bathed, dressed and bag in hand, she found Yorgos waiting to drive her to the ferry, her bewilderment increased.

Had she dreamed the night before? Had it all been just an extreme exercise in wish-fulfilment? Had she simply imagined that Alexis had told her that he loved her—not once, but so many times in that long and rapturous night? Had asked her to stay?

Because if it had been real, then where was he? And knew she could not ask.

'My wife is unwell,' Yorgos said awkwardly as he placed her bag in the car. 'But she wishes you a safe and pleasant journey, *thespinis.*'

Selena stared ahead of her, bleakly certain she'd been the subject of the earlier row. She swallowed.

'Please—thank her for…' She could hardly say *for making me welcome* or even *comfortable*, but managed, 'For looking after me.'

It was a silent journey, Selena battling with her increasingly unhappy thoughts and Yorgos clearly wrapped in his own worries.

When they arrived at the quayside, the ferry was just entering the harbour.

As Selena left the car, she reached for her bag but found that Yorgos had already retrieved it and was clutching it to him, with an air of mulish determination.

Her heart sank. She was clearly going to be put aboard the ferry, and he was going to wait until it had departed. It was like being deported, she thought, burning with embarrassment.

She summoned a smile from somewhere and held out her hand. 'I can manage, Yorgos. You don't need to stay.'

She was braced for an argument, but he said nothing, just stared past her, his expression turning to one of dismay.

Selena glanced round and saw Alexis standing a few feet away, hands on hips, his sunglasses pushed to the top of his head.

Their eyes met. As his smile reached out to her, she felt the bleak emptiness melt inside her.

'Kyria Blake is my responsibility, Yorgos.' His voice was quiet. 'You may return to the house.'

Yorgos muttered something, his shoulders slumped as he put down the bag, then got back in the car and drove away.

There was a silence, then Alexis said, 'So, *agapi mou*. Did you really think I would let you slip away, out of my life?'

She looked at him gravely. 'I wasn't sure. Millie told me that Eleni was upset earlier. I—I don't want to cause you more problems.'

He shrugged. 'There was a difference of opinion. At times, Eleni forgets I am no longer in the nursery. But it need not trouble you.'

He paused. 'Unless you really wish to go?'

Mutely, she shook her head. And let him take her hand in his and lead her away.

# CHAPTER NINE

HER HAND IN HIS, making her feel cherished. Safe and wanted, then and throughout the days and nights which followed.

But—above and beyond all—loved in a way she'd almost forgotten could exist, their mutual passion tempered with tenderness and consideration, her body free of its inhibitions flowering, opening to him at his touch.

And she was spoiled, too. Alexis had insisted on taking her on a shopping trip to Mykonos, and while Selena had refused to consider any of the more extreme fashions in the designer boutiques, she now had several bikinis with matching wraps, gorgeous silk shirts in jewel colours to wear with slim-fitting white pants and pretty dresses that floated like clouds for their evenings together.

Things he'd whispered that he would enjoy taking off and her smile told him she would enjoy that, too.

Most days they drove out together, lunching off freshly caught fish at small seaside *tavernas*, often returning to the Pillars of Apollo to make love in the drowsy heat of the afternoon. They often dined out in

the evenings, too, at places where there was traditional
Greek music and dancing in which Selena, in spite of
her initial protests, was made to join.

'You must learn, *matia mou*,' Alexis told her. 'So
you can dance at your sister's wedding.'

However, none of their rovings around the island,
including a tour round the ultra-modern, ultra-efficient
olive oil factory, took them back to the villa, confirm-
ing for Selena that she had indeed been concerned in
Alexis's 'difference of opinion' with Eleni, which troubled her. Instead, his apartment at the hotel had become
their own private domain, and if the staff there also dis-
approved of her presence, they hid it well, Stelios leading them in treating her with smiling courtesy.

Except for Kostas who seemed to be going out of his
way to avoid her.

She'd sought him out once to suggest that Millie
might join her occasionally beside the pool or on the
stretch of sandy beach below the hotel gardens, only to
receive a point blank refusal.

'You are the pillow friend of Kyrios Constantinou,
and that has caused more problems with my mother,'
he told her sullenly. 'It is better that my Amelia stays
away.'

She was tempted to remind him he was hardly in a
position to adopt the moral high ground, but decided
it would be more politic to keep quiet, telling herself
that things would sort themselves out. Although she
wasn't sure how.

The only time she was separated from Alexis was on

his trips to Athens when he would generally be away for at least twenty-four hours.

Selena missed him desperately during these brief absences, finding it difficult to sleep without his arms around her, and asked at one point if she could accompany him, but he'd refused. 'Athens is a sad place now, *agapi mou* and not always safe,' he told her gently and she'd reluctantly accepted his explanation.

However, when he warned her that his next trip would take much longer, lasting a week or more, she decided, instead of moping, to go back to Haylesford, not just for Millie's sake, but her own.

To break the news to Aunt Nora that she was putting her career plans on indefinite hold and returning to Rhymnos, and weathering the storm that would inevitably follow.

But Alexis seemed restive about the scheme. 'Wait a little, *matia mou*, until I can go with you,' he urged.

But Selena, under pressure from Millie, anxious about the date of her wedding, remained adamant.

'I can handle Aunt Nora,' she told him with more confidence than she actually felt. 'And I'll be back before you are.'

'You promise it?' he asked, his voice oddly sombre.

'Cross my heart,' she said. 'Besides, I have to go because Stelios did magic to get me on a flight and I can't let him down.'

His smile was thin. 'I must remember to thank him.'

'You do that,' she said and kissed him.

Yet the night preceding his departure, there was a fierce almost desperate edge to his lovemaking, which took her to new heights of pleasure but left her afterwards feeling forlorn to the point of sadness, even before they'd said goodbye.

And her mood wasn't lifted by the grey skies and rain that greeted her in England. By the time she reached her aunt's house from the station, she was chilled and damp.

And there was no one at home. She went into the kitchen and switched on the kettle, then went up to her room. The bed was freshly made up, indicating that her phone message had been received and she was expected, so presumably her aunt's absence was only temporary.

She ate a hasty meal of scrambled eggs on toast and drank two cups of coffee, then walked into town, first to the jewellers where Millie's bracelet was mended while she waited, then to the travel agency to book a return flight to Mykonos for the following day.

She was on her way back to the house when a girl's voice said, 'Hi, Selena,' and she turned to see Daisy and Fiona.

Just what I need, she thought, responding with a polite, 'Hello.'

'So, where's Millie?' Daisy looked around as if expecting her to pop out from behind a lamppost and shout *Boo*.

'On Rhymnos,' Selena said evenly. 'Preparing for her wedding.'

'Wedding?' Fiona echoed. 'How amazing. We thought she'd have had enough of the Greek stud scenario by now, didn't we, Dais?'

'Well—there you go,' Selena said briskly, trying to edge past them.

'So, in all this time, you didn't manage to talk her out of it,' said Daisy, and giggled. 'Or did you stay because you'd been talked into something yourself?'

Selena, to her annoyance, felt her colour rise but she managed a shrug. 'I think a career is a better choice. She doesn't.' She added, 'I'll tell her I saw you.'

'And make sure she invites us to the wedding,' Fiona called after her.

When pigs grow wings, Selena thought as she walked away. I'm not even sure I'll be invited myself, judging by the way Kostas spoke the other day.

'Pillow friend,' he'd called her, which sounded marginally better than 'mistress' or 'tart', but it meant the same and, knowing it had exposed her to the contempt of Anna Papoulis, stung like a thorn in her flesh.

And was painful in another way. Because it was so very far from 'wife'.

There, she thought, unhappily. I've said it at last. Faced the fact that in all this time, Alexis has never mentioned marriage. Never suggested that my staying with him should become permanent...

Or not in the way I've secretly hoped.

Perhaps he was just waiting until Millie and Kostas had their wedding. Or maybe not.

For a moment, she felt troubled, then pulled herself together as she remembered the warm, moonlit nights and his hands and mouth caressing her—arousing her. But above all, his voice whispering, *'S'agapo.'*

*I love you...*

And wasn't that what mattered? All that really mattered?

She sighed. If she said it enough times, she might even start to believe it.

Back at the house, she retrieved the 'Personal' file from the bottom drawer of her aunt's desk, extracting Millie's birth certificate and medical insurance documents and, after a moment's thought, her own, although, as she reminded herself firmly, it was unwise to make assumptions.

Now there were other practical matters to be considered, such as the contents of her wardrobe. She knew from Alexis that winters on Rhymnos could and probably would be cold, wet and stormy, so jeans and sweaters and her fleece would be useful. The rest could be bagged up for charity and she'd make a start on that now.

Because I can't wait to be out of here, she thought, hurling a blameless navy skirt into the reject sack. And back with the man I love, adding determinedly, on whatever terms.

She was just tying up the last sack when she heard a car arrive, then drive away and the rattle of a key in the front door.

Back from another little trip, she thought as she braced herself and went downstairs.

Aunt Nora was in the hall, removing her light waterproof jacket.

'So you're finally here,' she commented acidly. 'And Amelia with you, I trust.'

'Well, no, she isn't.' Selena forced a smile. 'You're looking well, Aunt Nora. I hope your leg has quite recovered.'

'It's still painful. I have to use a walking stick much of the time. So, where is your sister?'

Selena abandoned any further attempt at evasion. 'She's on Rhymnos,' she said. 'Planning her wedding. And she hopes you'll be one of her guests.'

There was an ominous silence. Then: 'So she intends to continue with this madness.' Aunt Nora drew a deep breath. 'Why did you allow this to happen, Selena—against my express wishes?'

'Because I couldn't prevent it.' Selena lifted her chin. 'And now I don't even want to. They love each other.' She paused. 'And there's something else you have to know. I've also met someone and tomorrow I'm going back to Rhymnos to be with him.'

Her aunt's voice shook with anger. 'You dare to say this to me—that you're throwing away your university place—the career I've offered—everything I've done for you? My God, your ingratitude is beyond belief.'

Selena said gently, 'I have tried to feel grateful, but somehow it never quite works. You want me to become a teacher, not for the good of the community, but to provide you with cheap labour at your expensive school. And I'd have done it, for Millie's sake. But she's decided her own future, setting me free to do the same.' She smiled. 'And I'm doing it. So if I do decide to teach, it will be on my terms.'

'Bold words,' said Miss Conway. 'Which you may well regret, my dear, when the summer's over and your boyfriend gets tired of you and throws you out. Or simply goes back to his wife.'

She paused. 'But you're right. Millie is a lost cause,

and I want nothing more to do with her or her Greek peasant. You, however, could still be of service to me, and when you discover you've made a terrible mistake, I might be prepared to give you another chance.'

Selena said woodenly, 'I'll bear it in mind.' But inwardly, she was still smarting over the wife comment.

Not that she believed her, of course. Yet there'd been times when she'd found Alexis watching her, his expression guarded. Other times when he'd seemed about to say something—but remained silent.

But when she'd queried this, his answer was invariably, 'I was thinking how very beautiful you are, *agapi mou.*'

Which was lovely to hear, but somehow left her still wondering…

Trust Aunt Nora to score a direct hit on my insecurity, she thought bitterly. And thank heaven she won't have many more opportunities.

It was cloudy but still hot when she reached Rhymnos. She'd left a message the previous day to let the hotel know she was returning, but no one had been there to meet her from the ferry, and she found herself transferring her heavy suitcase from hand to hand as she trudged up the hill.

There was no one at the desk when she walked in, so she headed straight for the lift, retrieving her key from her bag as she pressed the button.

Opening the door to the suite, she was immediately halted by the unexpected smell of cigar smoke, and as she paused, putting down her case, a large, powerfully built man in a crumpled cream linen suit, his dark hair streaked with grey, strolled out of the bedroom, a cheroot smouldering between be-ringed fingers.

At the same time, she realised there was another man, younger, thinner and wearing glasses, seated on one of the sofas with a briefcase beside him.

For an absurd moment, Selena thought she'd come to the wrong floor—the wrong room—and braced herself to back out apologising.

But then the man with the cigar spoke, his Greek accent spiked with transatlantic overtones. 'So you will be Miss Blake.'

Dark eyes under heavy grizzled brows swept her in a frank assessment that made her burn with embarrassment and indignation.

He turned to the other man. 'I can see the attraction, Manoli. That golden beauty and innocence combination would tempt a saint.' He sighed. 'And as we both know too well, my friend, my son is no saint.'

She found a voice. 'I'm sorry, but I don't understand.' She looked round almost wildly. 'Who are you—and where is Alexis?'

'My name is Petros Constantinou, and this is my family lawyer, Manoli Kerolas. As for Alexis...' He shrugged broad shoulders. 'He is in New York where he belongs and where he will remain from now on.' He gestured with the cigar. 'Now take a seat, young lady, while we discuss terms.'

'I prefer to stand.' Selena lifted her chin defiantly, aware that her heart was pounding and she felt deathly cold. 'And there is nothing to discuss.'

He sighed. 'As a favour to all of us, don't make this harder than it needs to be. Just accept that the party's over and get on with the rest of your life. Because you won't be seeing Alexis again, here or anywhere else. It's finished, *pethi mou*. Over.'

The words thudded into her like stones, and she forced herself not to flinch.

'I don't believe it,' she said. 'I'll never believe it until he tells me so himself.'

'That's not going to happen.' His tone was bluntly dismissive. 'My son's good at beginning things, but, as you've just found out, bad about ending them. He prefers that done for him. It's one of his weaknesses, I guess, like his attraction to willing blondes and his sentimental attachment to this island.

'But the olive oil project can run itself now, so he can devote himself to his neglected business and family duties in New York.'

He smiled. 'No doubt, marriage and fatherhood will at last encourage him to focus on what is important in his life, rather than trivial diversions, however attractive.'

'Marriage? Fatherhood?' Selena's throat was dry. 'What are you talking about?'

'Ah,' he said. 'You didn't know Alexis was about to be married?' He gave her a derisive look. 'But why would you spoil a beautiful romance by asking awkward questions?'

She said hoarsely, 'He wouldn't do this. He couldn't. He loves me.'

'I'm sure he told you so.' His voice was almost benign. 'Like most men, he would say anything to keep a pretty girl in his bed. But he is promised to a girl he has known since childhood, and the marriage will be celebrated almost immediately.'

He paused. 'In fact as soon as I have dealt with such extraneous matters as yourself, Miss Blake.' He beckoned to the lawyer. 'Now, in order to save my future daughter-in-law undeserved heartache, we need you to sign this.'

'What is it?' Her hands were clenched in the pockets of her jeans, her nails digging into her palms. Using one pain to fight another. Keeping it at bay until she could be alone.

His voice was hard. 'A legal undertaking that you will not contact my son again under any circumstances or disclose your past encounters with him here to any part of the media. In return for your agreement, I will arrange for two hundred and fifty thousand pounds sterling to be deposited in your bank account.'

He paused. 'Call it compensation for your disappointment, although I am sure you will have no difficulty in finding a new protector to replace Alexis.'

Selena said thickly, 'How—how bloody dare you! I won't sign a damned thing and you can keep your filthy money. But you don't have to worry.' She swallowed past the tightness in her throat. 'Do you really imagine I want to *think* about your son ever again, let alone *see* him or *talk* about him? If so, you must be mad.'

She indicated the door. 'Now perhaps you'll go.'

'This is Constantinou property, *thespinis*.' The lawyer spoke. 'It is for you to leave. Although you may first collect any clothing or gifts you received from Kyrios Alexis during your time together.'

She bent and retrieved her case. 'No.' Her voice shook. 'You can keep them, too.'

She added, 'I want nothing from any of you—not now—not ever.'

And managed, somehow, without stumbling or yielding to the pain and grief waiting to swamp her, to turn and walk away.

As she emerged from the lift, her legs shaking under her, she saw Kostas standing in the doorway of the bar and managed to remember the errand that had sent her back to England.

She took the envelope containing the documents and the bracelet from her bag and handed it to him, somehow keeping her voice even. 'For Millie.'

His glance slid away. He said hurriedly, 'I am sorry for this trouble that has come to you,' and went back into the bar.

After that, it all became ridiculously simple. The ferry was still loading at the quayside, and when she reached the airport on Mykonos there was an empty seat on a late afternoon flight.

It was almost as if the Fates, too, were conspiring to be rid of her.

She bought a ticket for Haylesford because she could think of nothing else to do.

Knowing there was nothing she could say in her own defence that could possibly justify this sordid, hideous little episode.

That she'd gone willingly and, above all, unquestioningly into the arms of a man about to marry his child-hood sweetheart, who had used her and now, cynically ditched her, without even the courage to face her himself with the truth.

Just because he'd told her he loved her and she had wanted so desperately to believe him…

Not an excuse, she realised, that would cut any ice with her aunt, even if she could bring herself to use it. And she could just imagine the grim triumph that would greet it.

As the train pulled into Stilbury, the stop before Haylesford, obeying an imperative she barely understood, she grabbed her case and got out.

She walked into the town, found a cheap hotel and took a room for the night. The next day, she emptied her bank account for the advance rent on a tiny bedsit, and took a job as a waitress in a busy gastropub, full-time and with long hours but her own tips.

Not great, she thought, but work. Because work was the answer. The magic formula that would let her forget Greece and everything that had happened there.

And perhaps, at that desperate moment, she even believed it might be possible.

# CHAPTER TEN

YET HERE SHE WAS, on board the ferry once again as it approached Rhymnos, the heat of the rail burning through her clothes as she leaned against it, her hands clenched in tense fists at her sides.

Up to the moment when she'd boarded the plane, she'd told herself that she didn't have to do this. That there was still time to change her mind. But the chance of a rapprochement with Millie had decided her.

Kostas said things had changed, she thought, and he was right. The harbour had been enlarged, and smart motor yachts now outnumbered the fishing boats.

She made herself look past them at the white building on the hill, hoping against hope that this might have been transformed, altered beyond recognition, or, preferably, demolished, its associations buried with it.

Knowing, at the same time, that she couldn't be that lucky. That there wasn't even the palliative of a board announcing 'Under New Ownership'.

Kostas was waiting when she disembarked and insisted on carrying her bag. 'I am thankful to see you, sister. My Amelia will be so happy.'

His *taverna* was at the far end of the harbour, clean and colourful with its tubs of geraniums and red and white awning. Obviously busy, too, with all the outside tables taken.

Heaven alone knew how he'd raised the money to acquire it, she thought in bewilderment, but the gamble seemed to have paid off.

They went through the bar into the kitchen where Anna Papoulis was lifting a large dish of moussaka from one of the ovens, her normally sour expression deepening when she saw Selena, while totally ignoring her polite, *'Kalimera.'*

No change there, then, Selena thought wryly, following Kostas through a curtained doorway and up a flight of wooden stairs to the first floor.

Her room, situated at the end of a narrow passage and overlooking a rear yard with bins and crates, was small and little more than basic, with a low bed, covered by a thin red blanket, a narrow cupboard for her belongings and a rag rug on the hastily swept floor.

Ah well, she thought, I'm not planning a long stay. Only to remember, with a sudden pang of alarm, that was what she'd said the first time she came to Rhymnos, and how disastrously that had turned out.

But that was then, she reminded herself. This was now, and she was a different person.

Kostas deposited her bag on the bed and gave her an anxious look. 'You will come to my poor Amelia?'

'That's what I'm here for.' She kept her voice upbeat and even managed a reassuring smile.

But the smile slipped a bit when she followed Kostas

along the passage to the main bedroom and found his poor Amelia in a pretty blue dressing gown reclining in the middle of a very large bed, with a dish containing a half-eaten bunch of grapes beside her and clearly as far from death's door as anyone wearing mascara and lip gloss could possibly be.

'Oh.' She put down the magazine she'd been reading.

'So here you are. I'd begun to think you'd changed your mind.' Her eyes widened. 'What the hell have you done to your hair?'

'Cut it,' said Selena. 'Hello, Mills.'

She walked across and sat on the edge of the bed. 'I thought you were ill.'

Millie grimaced. 'I am. I've never felt so dreadful in my entire life. I can't stop being sick, but I get no sympathy from the old bat downstairs. She seems to think I should still be waiting on tables. It would serve her right if I threw up over the customers.'

She added, 'That's one of the reasons I wanted you here, because I thought you'd understand.' And paused. 'Or perhaps you were one of the lucky ones and didn't get sick.'

The room was hot, but Selena felt icy cold. *One of the lucky ones...*

She tried to speak steadily. 'Millie, are you telling me you're pregnant?'

'Yes, of course. Naturally, Kostas is turning cartwheels, but then he doesn't have to suffer like this.' She took another grape. 'Fruit is all I can eat. It's a nightmare.'

No, thought Selena, her throat closing. I'm the one

having the nightmare. After everything that's happened, how can she be doing this to me?

She got to her feet. 'I believe morning sickness usually ends after the first trimester, unless you're very unlucky. In any event, it's hardly an emergency.' She walked towards the door. 'I hope all goes well for you.'

'Where are you going?'

'Back to the UK. Where else?' Selena's tone was crisp.

'But you've only just got here,' Millie protested. 'Besides, it isn't just the baby, Lena.' She was kneeling on the bed, her voice faltering and sounding very young. 'We have big, big problems and we need your help.'

Of course they did, thought Selena, unease crawling across her skin like the scrape of a nail on glass.

Every instinct was screaming, was telling her to go, yet she found herself hesitating. She said, 'I presume it's about money. Yet the *taverna* seems to be doing well.'

'It is. Which makes everything so much worse.'

'What does?'

Millie's face was flushed, her eyes tearful. 'To know we've been cheated. And that we may lose it all—our home—our living—everything.'

And she threw herself, sobbing, against her pillows.

Selena came back to the bed. 'Don't, Millie,' she said gently. 'You need to keep calm—for the baby's sake,' she added, stumbling a little over the words. 'Now, tell me how you've been cheated.'

Her sister gulped. 'The *taverna* didn't belong to the guy who made the deal with Kostas, and now the real owner wants it back.'

Selena stared at her in genuine shock. 'Surely your lawyer should have picked up on any query over the title?'

Millie looked away. 'It was all handled privately. We didn't have a lawyer.'

'Well, you need one now,' Selena said briskly, wondering if Kostas was certifiable.

Millie still wasn't looking at her. She said in a low voice, 'We hoped you'd help us.'

'But that's ridiculous.' Selena spread her hands in exasperation. 'I'm going to be a teacher. I haven't a clue about Greek or any other kind of law.'

'But if you talked to the owner, you might persuade him to change his mind.'

'Why on earth should he listen to me?'

And, as if from a far distance, she heard Millie say, 'Because it's Alexis Constantinou. He's back, staying at the hotel and he wants to see you.'

'You lied to me. Both of you. How could you do that?'

She faced the pair of them, her body rigid, her mind still reeling under the shock of it. The agony of another betrayal...

Millie looked at her beseechingly. 'If we'd told you the truth, you wouldn't have come. And we're desperate. We have nowhere else to turn.'

'Then nothing's changed.' Selena's tone bit. 'I won't see him.' And then ruined it by asking, 'Is he alone?'

Kostas looked at the floor. 'Here—yes. Elsewhere? Who knows?'

*Who indeed?* Pain struck at her again, harsh and

deep, telling her all her attempts at putting the past behind her had been totally in vain. As if she was still the naïve, gullible idiot who'd believed everything he'd told her.

Who'd even dared to dream…

Until, of course, his father had ripped off her rose-tinted spectacles and revealed Alexis for what he truly was…

She said slowly, 'Are you sure it's him and not his father asking for me?'

'What has his father to do with it?' asked Millie. Kostas, however, remained silent.

He looks almost guilty, thought Selena, although being an idiot was hardly a criminal offence or even a mortal sin.

But, having arranged to have her cut so brutally from his life, why was Alexis now trying to force her into another confrontation?

This threat to ruin Kostas and Millie was placing her in an impossible predicament.

If she refused to see Alexis, he would win. In fact, the offer of negotiation had to be a deliberate ploy on his part. He knew exactly what her reaction would be, and he could assign the blame to her if Kostas and Millie became homeless.

But she would not allow that to happen, she told herself with icy purpose. She could not let him think she was too scared—too broken to face him. If all she had was pride to carry her through, then she would make it enough.

She said quietly, 'Don't cry any more, Mills. It's bad

for the baby. And—yes—I'll talk to him if that's what it takes, but I promise nothing. I'm quite sure he has his own agenda.'

She looked back at Kostas who was still avoiding her gaze. 'Has he mentioned a time and place?'

He cleared his throat. '*Ochi.* Not yet.'

Instinct told Selena that there was obviously more to this than met the eye, but at the moment she had enough to cope with.

'Right.' She moved to the door. 'Now I think I'll have a shower and relax for a while. OK?'

And on their subdued murmur of assent, she left them to it.

The shower was refreshing, but there was no question of relaxation afterwards.

She still could hardly believe what was happening, or why. Was unable to credit how Alexis could have the gall to treat her like this—to add insult to the terrible injury he'd already inflicted.

Proof if proof were needed that he'd never cared for her, she thought, fighting the wave of pain and grief that threatened once more to overwhelm her.

That all the warmth and tenderness he'd shown her had simply been a ploy to entice her, pliant and, above all, unquestioning, into his bed, and keep her to provide him with sexual entertainment until his real world claimed him back, and he could simply walk away.

He must have known how she felt. Had it amused him to make her admit she'd surrendered her heart as well as her body?

Had this ruthless pursuit of his own pleasure always

been there, under the charm and allure, only she'd been too besotted to see it?

And perhaps Eleni's forbidding attitude had been an attempt to warn her away before too much harm was done?

She must have asked herself these questions a thousand, thousand times, until she'd finally decided it was time she stopped looking for answers and—moved on. Or as much as she could under the circumstances. She'd thought she was succeeding.

Yet here she was, once again in torment. Knowing that her wounds were still raw.

Among the many things, she realised, her throat tightening, that she needed to keep hidden when, eventually, she had to face him again. Most of all, the precious photograph now propped against the bottle of water on the rickety bedside table.

She picked it up and studied it, her heart clenching in tenderness in response to the small, laughing face with the lively dark eyes.

'Not long now, darling,' she said softly. 'And we'll be together always—and that's a promise.' She kissed the photograph and put it back on the table.

She would not wait, cowering, to be summoned, she decided. Tomorrow, she would take matters into her own hands and go to Alexis. Let him know he had a fight on his hands.

Pleading tiredness after her flight, she went to bed early, intending to plan some kind of strategy.

But it was hard to concentrate as she lay naked under the single sheet, listening to the sounds of *bouzouki* wafting up from the *taverna*, and remembering, in spite of herself, the long evenings of eating, drinking and music under the stars.

How she'd clapped her hands to the rhythm as she watched Alexis dance with the other men, more grace-ful, more virile than any of his companions, before she and the rest of the girls were summoned to form a long line with the men, laughing and breathless as they dipped, swayed and spun between the tables in sim-ple, uncomplicated happiness.

How, later, in his arms, her body had moved to a very different rhythm. Been urged to a pleasure so deep it was almost pain.

And became aware, with shame that her body was stirring at the memory, her nipples hardening against the linen that covered them.

She turned over, pressing her face into the hard pil-low.

'Damn him.' Her whisper ached in the darkness. 'Damn him to hell.'

'So,' Selena said briskly. 'What I need from you is paperwork—something to prove that you bought the *taverna* in good faith, and that you might be due some compensation.'

'We don't want compensation,' said Millie. 'Just to keep the Amelia. Besides, I don't think there is any paperwork. Kostas says it was a private arrangement.'

'He told me the same thing.' Selena gave her sister a level look. 'Mills, I really need to know what you and Kostas aren't telling me.'

'There's nothing, honestly.' Millie was clearly bewildered. She got to her feet. 'I'm going shopping before it gets too hot. We want some more cucumbers.'

Selena stopped her. 'I'll get them on my way back. You stay in the shade and rest.'

'You are sure about this?' Millie subsided into her chair again. 'Wouldn't it be better to wait until he sends for you?'

'Not from where I'm standing.' Selena smiled at her. 'Stop worrying.'

She set off along the waterfront and up the hill to the hotel, just as she'd done that first time all those months ago.

Stelios was at reception when she walked in. He looked up and smiled. 'Kyria Blake.'

She made herself smile back at him, easily and confidently. '*Kalimera*, Stelios. Is the boss around? I really need to speak to him. But if he's busy I can come back later.'

*But will I? Or, if I wait, will I lose whatever reserve of courage brought me here and run...? Except I can't do that. I have to go through with it now, whatever happens.*

'No, no, he will see you now.' Stelios reached for the internal telephone. 'He has been expecting you.'

Yes, she thought. Of course. What else did I think? But now the fight begins.

She stood beside him in the lift, carefully unclenching her hands, and making herself breathe slowly and evenly. Reminding herself why she was there. Rehearsing in her head what she had to say.

Reminding herself that she was here to confront her demons and conquer them at last.

'Kyrios Alexis is having breakfast,' Stelios informed her as he unlocked the door to the apartment and ushered her inside.

She nodded. *'Efharisto.'*

*'Parakalo,'* he returned and backed out, closing the door behind him.

She crossed the empty sitting room and went into the bedroom, deliberately averting her eyes from the unmade bed.

The long windows stood open and Alexis, barefoot and barelegged in a white towelling robe which emphasised the deep bronze of his skin, was sitting at the table on the balcony, drinking coffee, the remains of his meal—fruit, fresh bread and cherry jam—pushed to one side.

She walked slowly forward and he looked round, staring at her, his eyes narrowing.

His face seemed thinner, she thought, its features more deeply accentuated. And, above all, tired.

*'Kalimera.'* He indicated the chair on the other side of the table. 'Would you like coffee?'

She sat. 'There's only one cup.'

'How can that matter,' he said softly, 'when we have already shared so much?'

Clearly, he was not going to make this easy for her.

She met the mockery in his eyes. 'But not,' she said, 'for some time.'

'Yet you are here now. Allow me to express my pleasure.'

Selena lifted her chin. 'To negotiate,' she said crisply. 'Nothing else.'

'Nothing? I fear you must think again.'

And suddenly, every word she had planned to say, every careful argument she'd devised, went out of her head.

Instead she heard herself asking the question she'd promised herself would remain taboo. 'Why didn't you tell me you were going to be married?'

He said levelly, 'Because I hoped it would not be necessary.'

While she was still reeling from this, he added, 'Why have you cut off your hair?'

*Hair like moonlight...*

She pulled herself together. 'Convenience.'

'No,' he said with sudden harshness. 'Sacrilege.'

She had a sudden memory of the hairdresser saying anxiously, 'Are you quite sure?' How, she'd nodded silently, then sat looking down at her hands, clenched in her lap, as the shining silver-blonde lengths fell to the floor.

She took a deep breath. 'Perhaps we should turn to the problem of the Taverna Amelia.'

'The difficulties of your sister and her worthless husband can wait. I used them only as an excuse to bring you here.' His smile chilled her. 'We have the matter of a personal debt to discuss—you and I.'

'What debt?' Selena shook her head. 'I—I don't understand.'

'You owe me a child, Selene *mou*,' he said softly. 'Or did you think I would not find out?'

She stared back at him, hardly able to breathe, her whole body rigid with shock.

How could he know? she asked herself desperately. How had he found out that she'd been pregnant? Or what had become of the baby since?

At the same time realising that it was not tension she had seen in his face but anger. And directed, unbelievably, at her.

'I—I don't know what you mean.' She could barely recognise her own voice.

'Do not lie to me, *matia mou*—my eyes—my beautiful, shining, innocent eyes.' His voice was harsh, his face inimical. 'Eyes that made me believe that it might be possible at last to love—to trust. What a fool I was.'

He paused. 'Tell me—was it my son or my daughter—the child you gave away so carelessly to strangers?'

Oh, God, how could he do this? Describe in such terms the hardest decision she'd ever taken in her life?

'Alexis,' she said desperately. 'Alexis—you must listen to me...'

'I am listening. Waiting for an answer to my question. Boy or girl?'

'A boy.' She bent her head, her throat tightening uncontrollably. Terrified in case she broke down in front of him—this bitter stranger.

*When he was born, they had to sedate me because I was hysterical—unable to stop crying—calling out for you... While afterwards I was alone, having to concentrate on simply staying alive—keeping body and soul together somehow, when really I wanted to die myself.*

She looked at him, afraid of what he might see. She said dully, 'If that's what you wanted to know, may I go now, please?'

'You will leave when I permit you to go. Not before.'

She glanced up, startled, at that and felt his smile scrape across her senses.

He added, 'You see, Selena *mou*, I require you to remain here with me until you have given me another child, to replace the one you were so quick to abandon. And, in that way, paid your debt to me in full. Do I make myself clear?'

# CHAPTER ELEVEN

THE DISTANCE BETWEEN them seemed to have widened—become impassable. Terrifying.

She said hoarsely, 'You don't—you can't mean it. Alexis—the past is gone and we can't change it—any of it. We have to look to the future—get on with the lives we've chosen.' She added with difficulty, 'With the—the people we've chosen.'

'You refer to your man in England?' His gaze rested sardonically on her bare hands. 'If he is still in your life, he seems in no hurry to marry you.'

And now was not the time to admit there was no such person nor ever had been, she thought.

She lifted her chin. 'No,' she said clearly. 'I was speaking of your wife.'

'I have no wife,' he said.

'Oh.' She paused. 'You're divorced?' *Why was she even asking?*

'No,' he said. 'There was no divorce, because there was never a marriage. I broke off the engagement.'

She said huskily, 'I—I don't understand.'

He shrugged. 'I do not require your understanding,

Selena *mou*, only your cooperation as I think I have made clear.'

She rose. 'And I came here solely to discuss the legal problem over the ownership of Taverna Amelia and try to reach a settlement.'

'Sit down,' he said. 'And listen to me.' He waited until she unwillingly resumed her seat. 'There is no problem. Kostas knows the *taverna* and the land it stands on belongs to me. And I want it back.'

She fought her dismay. Tried to sound confident. 'Then, at some point, he's been misled. And at least he deserves the purchase price repaid.'

His glance was derisive. 'You are the one who has been misled, Selena *mou*, because he paid nothing. And now you are here to induce me to be merciful, and withdraw eviction proceedings against him and his pregnant wife.' He paused, adding sardonically, 'You are a fertile family, it seems.'

Best to ignore that, she thought, biting savagely into her lip. 'But Kostas worked for you. You encouraged him to marry Millie. Why have you turned against him?'

'Once again, you are mistaken. It was Kostas who turned against me.'

Selena stifled a groan. I knew it, she thought. Knew there was something very wrong.

She said carefully, 'But why should he do that?'

'He imagined that marrying your sister would give him some kind of privileged standing with me.' His shrug was cynical. 'I had to show him he was wrong. He decided to take his revenge.' His mouth tightened. 'A great mistake.'

She bit her lip. 'Am I allowed to know what he did?'

He shrugged. 'Why not—as it also concerns you.'

'Me?'

'Of course,' he said. 'What other weapon did he have? He had somehow learned of my engagement and that my father was pressing me to honour the arrangement and marry the girl.'

'Your childhood sweetheart,' she said.

'Never.' His tone was scornful. 'But what is one more lie among so many? I had indeed met her once or twice as a child. Her father, Ari Sofiakis, was a business colleague of my father's in the early days of the Constantinou Corporation.

'Katerina was her father's princess, spoiled, whining and detestable and the intervening years had not improved her. Her interests in life were fashion magazines, chocolates and cosmetic surgery. I doubt we had a thought in common.'

'Then why did you agree to marry her?'

'I did not. It was put to me as a done deal and I refused absolutely. At first my father argued that this would deeply offend the Sofiakis family, and I retorted he should have obtained my consent before proceeding.

'And then he told me the truth. That, years before, he had made corrupt payments to civic officials in order to secure lucrative contracts for our companies. That Ari Sofiakis knew of this and my marriage to Katerina was now the price of his silence.

'By this time, you see, he had realised that other potential bridegrooms for his precious child were being deterred by the stories of her extravagance and temper tantrums and he was becoming desperate to find her a rich husband.

'Unless I complied, he, my own father, would end up in court and almost certainly go to jail, which would be a catastrophe for Constantinou International and, by association for me, his only son.'

She said shakily, 'But that's blackmail on both sides.'

'Of course.' He shrugged. 'I was presented with two intolerable choices, and I chose reluctantly to protect my father, and agreed to an engagement.

'But the wedding, I made clear, must wait. I had already committed myself to trying to protect Rhymnos from the worst effects of the economic crisis and nothing would change that.

'But I told the Sofiakis family that if Katerina would agree to a small, hasty wedding, she was welcome to accompany me to the island and share whatever privations that might involve.'

He added casually, 'It was a safe offer. Katerina, I knew, would never willingly travel further from Manhattan than the Hamptons or Cape Cod and after both she and her mother had indulged in a series of increasingly hysterical scenes, the marriage was safely postponed.

'Before my departure, I hired a team of investigators to take a close look at Ari Sofiakis. I wasn't hopeful. He had a reputation for utter probity in his business life and was known as a religious man and a major donor to charity.

'At the same time, I had my lawyers and accountants working in the background to make me totally indepen-

dent from Constantinou International.' His voice was
expressionless. 'I had learned my lesson.'

She said, 'And your investigators found something?'

'Yes,' he said. 'When I had almost given up hope. In
his charity work. One small, insignificant organisation,
run by an order of nuns, helping potential immigrants
to adapt to life in the US, and supported regularly and
generously by Mr Sofiakis and a number of his friends
and other prominent members of the community.' He
paused. 'Which did not include my father.

'The team found this—odd. When they looked
deeper, they found the nuns long gone and their house
sold. While the immigrants, most of them illegal, but
all female and beautiful, were high-class and expensive
call-girls with Ari a faithful and long-standing client.

'They telephoned me in Athens with the news and I
flew straight to New York to confront him, not knowing my father, under pressure from his family, had also
been busy. Mr Sofiakis agreed to end the engagement
but then had to invent some reason to placate his wife
and daughter. I almost felt sorry for him.'

His mouth hardened. 'Until my father told me that
my relationship with you was over, too, and I should
turn my attention to finding myself another bride from
our community.'

'When I said I would marry you or no one, he advised me not to waste my time. That you were a greedy
tramp who had let yourself be bought off for a quarter
of a million pounds.

'His lawyer even produced a document you had
signed, promising to give me up, and congratulated

me on my "lucky escape".' He pronounced the words
with distaste.

She said numbly, 'And you believed them?'

'Not my father, perhaps,' he said. 'But I had no reason then to doubt Manoli. I had been at college with his
younger brother, and looked on his family as friends.'

'Whereas I was just a pillow friend,' she said scornfully. 'One of many, no doubt.'

'If you expect me to apologise for my past, Selene
*mou*, you will be disappointed.'

Their glances met—clashed—and she was the first
to look away.

'How did you discover the truth—about the money?'

'Months later, when my father unwisely fired Manoli.
By then I had separated myself from Constantinou International, and offered him a job. He broke down and
confessed you had rejected the pay off, and that my father had signed the document in your name, gambling
rightly on my not recognising your signature and being
too shocked to question its validity.

'I told him the job offer stood and booked an immediate flight to England, to find you.' He paused. 'In the
town where your aunt has a school.'

Her head went back. She said hoarsely, 'You saw
Aunt Nora?'

'Yes,' he said. 'And heard her, too. How you had refused her help, her offers of support. How your hatred
of me had caused you to reject our baby at birth.

'Some might say I owe Kostas thanks for putting an
end to my illusions about you,' he added bitterly. 'But
somehow I cannot be grateful.'

Her head swam. She felt herself gulping in air, struggling not to fall to pieces after this new blow. Because she needed to concentrate her energies on finding a way out of this nightmare.

Not unscathed—she would carry his anger, his accusations with her like a scar—but hopefully with her self-respect still intact.

'Yet you still used him to bring me here.' Her voice was brittle.

'If you'd known I had sent for you, would you have agreed?' He watched her look away and nodded. 'I thought not.'

But was that the truth? How many times had she imagined standing before him—asking the questions that haunted her?

I can never tell him that, she thought achingly, because I dare not let him see that the answers to those questions still matter to me.

That, God help me, he still matters—in spite of everything...

She said, 'So, I have to tell Kostas that he's lost his home and his living.'

'I think, Selena *mou*, that he already knows.' He shrugged again. 'His time on Rhymnos is done.'

He paused, watching her, his eyes lingering on her mouth. 'And now shall we turn to our more personal negotiations?'

'There is nothing to discuss.' She looked back defiantly. 'I have no intention of—co-operating as you put it. The idea disgusts me—as it should you.'

'Such indignation,' he returned softly. 'Yet I am only

being practical. I am a single man who needs an heir. I require you to provide one for me. If I had known you had already done so, I would have induced you to hand him over to me, instead of hastily abandoning him to strangers.'

She said thickly, 'I—did not—abandon him. Before he was born, I was living in one room, able only to work part-time and receiving benefits.' She swallowed. 'It took me longer than it should have to—recover—afterwards, and that's when he was taken to—to live with another family.'

'You did not think to contact me—his father?'

'No, because I thought—I'd been told—that by then you'd be married. I—I didn't want to intrude on your new life.'

'How noble.' He studied her through half-closed eyes. 'And how much you must have regretted refusing my father's money.'

'Never,' she said. 'Not for one moment.'

'You were content to simply—let your baby go?'

*Content? If hearts could break twice, mine would have done so.*

She kept her voice steady. 'The decision was made for me.'

'How convenient,' he drawled. 'Then let me tell you what I have decided. That you shall become, in effect, a surrogate mother. After the birth, I shall legally adopt the child, son or daughter, leaving you to walk away unencumbered once again. Although I shall naturally pay for your services.'

She stared at him, shaking with disbelief—and with

her own mounting anger as it mingled with the renewed pain at his treatment of her.

'How generous.' Her voice vibrated with scorn. 'But I do hope you're not offering another paltry two hundred and fifty thousand as your father did. My starting price would be at least double that amount.'

There was a long, taut silence. Apart from the sudden clench of a muscle in his jaw, he was motionless, his dark eyes studying her as if he had never seen her before.

'So,' he said eventually. 'You have actually managed to surprise me, Selene *mou*. But at least we now know where we stand. And I will pay whatever you ask, although I advise you not to allow your greed to run away with you. Do we have a deal?'

She drew a quick, harsh breath. 'No,' she said raggedly. 'We do not and we never will, you—you unutterable bastard. How could you even think so?' A sob she could not control rose in her throat, as she pushed back her chair and stood up. 'I think you're utterly vile and despicable—and I only wish to God that I'd never met you.'

He, too, got to his feet, taking a step towards her, bringing him too close for comfort—or safety. Making her dizzily aware of the warm, familiar scent of his skin.

Reviving memories that were poignant as well as dangerous.

'Truly?' His voice was harsh. 'I wish I could feel the same—but, even now, I cannot.'

If he came any closer she would be lost and she knew it.

Stay calm, she whispered silently. And walk away.

But when she reached the outer door he was beside her, his hand on her arm.

She recoiled. She said between her teeth, 'Do—not—touch me.'

'Forgive me, but there is something I must know.' There was a strange, almost anguished note in his voice. 'My son—what is his name?'

The empty passage ahead of her became a sudden blur, but she forced back the tears.

She said huskily, 'Alexander.' And fled.

'You,' she said. 'You dared to ask for my help, when you knew what you'd done? When you'd ruined my life?'

They were alone in the bar. Millie was resting upstairs and Madame Papoulis, muttering, had gone to buy the forgotten cucumbers.

Kostas's face was wretched. 'I was angry, sister, because I asked Kyrios Alexis to lend me money to buy my business and he refused me. He said that if I wished to marry, I should work and save for my wife, not borrow what I might not be able to repay.'

He hit his chest with a clenched fist. 'In that moment, he made me feel less than a man, and I wished to make him sorry.

'At his house, I had heard Eleni and Yorgos talking when they did not know I was there, speaking of the marriage in America arranged for him by his father. How there would be great trouble if Kyrios Petros found out that Kyrios Alexis had a pillow friend who had taken his eyes and his heart.'

She winced. 'So you told him.'

'*Ne*. And he promised I would be rewarded. I only wanted the money Kyrios Alexis had refused, but he offered me this *taverna*, which was not his to give. He cheated me.'

She said icily, 'I hope you don't expect sympathy.'

'I expect nothing. My life is finished.' He looked up pleadingly. 'Please, sister, do not tell my Amelia that I am to blame for our loss. I cannot bear for her to know.'

'I think she'd prefer honesty,' she said crisply.

'And it might be best if I caught the afternoon ferry.' *In case Alexis comes looking for me.*

Just the thought made her throat tighten in a mixture of panic and desolation.

'But if you leave like this, your sister will wonder.' He gave her another beseeching look. 'For her sake, stay a little longer.'

'Until tomorrow,' she said stonily. 'Then I'm gone.'

'I am thankful.' He sighed. 'I hoped you would persuade Kyrios Alexis to forgive me, so that my Amelia and I can keep our dream.'

*And what about my dream—my hopes—my loss?* she wanted to scream at him. *And the price I paid—that I'm still paying? That I only get to see my little boy once a week, and at the occasional weekend. That now his foster parents are talking about adoption, and I shall have to fight to keep him.*

She took a deep breath. 'I think you'll just have to buckle down and—start again—somewhere else.' She got up from the table. 'I'll see if Millie's asleep.'

Not just asleep, but dead to the world, she thought as

she peeped round the door. She went to her own room, and sat on the edge of the bed, staring into space.

Her meeting with Alexis had left her sick and shaking inwardly. Would it have been easier to endure, she wondered, if they'd met on neutral territory, instead of somewhere still charged with memories?

Their bedroom, she thought achingly, its balcony overlooking the lawns and the sea beyond, rippling to the edge of the beach in its own quiet, endless rhythm, and where, at night, she would watch the moon carving her silver path across the water.

The room, too, where one warm, golden afternoon their baby had been conceived...

She remembered waking from a delicious dream and reaching for him to find the space beside her unoccupied. She slid naked from the bed and went to find him.

He was in the bathroom, his dark hair still damp from the shower, standing at a basin, a towel draped round his hips, deftly removing the last traces of lather from his chin with his razor.

He saw her in the mirror and smiled, the glint in his eyes showing his appreciation for the provocative picture she made, framed in the doorway.

Selena walked across and slid her arms round his waist, pressing her face against the warm skin of his bare back, breathing the scent of his soap, and marking the length of his supple spine with small, soft kisses.

She unfastened his towel and let it fall to the floor, her hands sweeping slowly down over the taut male buttocks to the muscular length of his thighs.

She heard him gasp softly then the rattle of the razor slipping from his fingers into the basin. His body tensing under her caress, he leaned forward, his head bent and his hands gripping the edge of the tiled surround.

Her lips moved downward, tantalising him with every kiss, her teeth grazing him gently as she slid a hand between his legs, cupping him, teasing him with her fingertips, then reaching for his rigid, straining shaft and stroking it until he groaned aloud.

He turned, lifting her as if she was featherweight, then lowering her on to his loins and filling her with one smooth thrust.

Selena clung to him, arms round his neck, her legs wrapped round his hips. Their mouths were locked together, their tongues tangling, in a silence broken only by the rasp of their breathing and the sound of flesh against flesh as she rode him, demanding, challenging in her glorious abandonment, her muscles gripping him, urging him on, taking him deeper and deeper still.

The harsh, exquisite ascent to pleasure was already building inside her, surging towards its peak, then overwhelming her, convulsing her in such an agony of delight that she cried out into his mouth.

And in the next instant felt him explode, his climax white-hot within her.

Afterwards, they found their way, somehow, to the bed and lay for a while, exchanging quiet kisses.

Eventually, Alexis lifted himself on to an elbow and looked down at her, stroking a strand of hair back from her sweat-dampened face.

He said slowly, half to himself, 'I did not intend that.'

It was unexpected and she gave him a questioning, almost anxious glance. 'Are you sorry?'

'No,' he said, and kissed her again. 'No, my beautiful one, my angel, I could never be that.' His smile was faintly rueful. 'But I meant to be wise for us both.'

And only some weeks later, when she first began to feel sick in the mornings, did she realise, as he must have done at the time, that it was the only time they'd had unprotected sex.

Which had left her to face, totally alone, the most terrifying, heart-wrenching moments of her life...

# CHAPTER TWELVE

'GO BACK AND talk to him again, Lena, please. Say whatever you have to, but make him listen.' Millie looked dreadful, her face pale, her eyes swollen. 'After all, he was crazy about you once. Everyone knew it.'

Selena bit her lip. She had agreed with Kostas to tell her sister that she'd tried to reason with Alexis, but that he'd remained totally intransigent.

Her worry that Alexis might come to the Amelia to repeat his offer in person had proved unfounded, but that was the only positive in the day so far.

She said briskly, 'What's past is gone, Mills, and we have to accept that. And downstairs there is a full house wanting dinner. So, do something about your face then come down and charm the customers before your mother-in-law has a total fit.'

'What's the point?' Millie asked despairingly. 'When we're about to lose everything anyway.'

Selena stood up. She said evenly, 'Because you're facing a fresh start and for that you'll need every penny you can make, including tips.' Adding, 'As I once did.'

* * *

When she got downstairs next morning, she found Kostas, looking heavy-eyed, sweeping the *taverna* floor.

He saw the bag she was carrying and frowned. 'You are truly leaving?'

'I did say so.'

'But the manager at the hotel brought this for you.' He went to the bar and produced an envelope. 'I hoped it might be from Kyrios Alexis saying he had thought again.'

'I think the age of miracles is past.' She took the envelope and went outside to read it, aware Kostas was watching anxiously from the doorway.

The note was brief. 'The deal I offered is no longer on the table and you have nothing further to fear from me. I wish you well.' And his initial.

'Does he want to see you again?' asked Kostas.

'No,' she said. 'He's—just saying goodbye.'

She read it again, her heart thumping, asking herself what could have prompted this total *volte face*.

Well—practical considerations, probably. One day, he would meet someone he wanted to marry, and an adopted child born from a supposed surrogate mother in another country would require too much explanation.

Or had he simply decided to take 'no' for an answer?

She thought—*It's over. I'm free.*

So, why wasn't she jumping for joy?

Worse still, why did she feel suddenly so lost—so scared?

Because I have a tough time ahead, she told herself. I have to find an affordable two-bedroom flat where children are allowed, then let the authorities know I'm in steady full-time employment, and that Alexander no longer needs fostering and should be living with me.

After all, I've already missed out on too much of his babyhood...

And paused, biting her lip. Because, it occurred to her with all the force of a blow, she was not the only one.

I can't do this, she thought. Whatever Alexis thinks of me, I can't walk away and leave him with—nothing.

She folded the note and put it in her shoulder bag. She said, 'Can I leave my other things here, Kostas? There's something I need to do before I go.'

Stelios was standing on the terrace in front of the hotel, talking to an elderly couple. As they departed, he turned to her, his smile fading, his tone formal. 'Kyria Blake. How may I help you?'

She said, 'I need to see him. Will you tell him it's important—please?'

'He is not here, *thespinis*. Last night, he went back to his house, and later today he leaves for Athens.' He added flatly, 'I do not know when he will return to Rhymnos.'

'His house?' she echoed, reckoning up the cash she had with her. 'Then can you get me a taxi?'

He looked at her in astonishment. 'There is only one on the island, *thespinis*. It belongs to Takis, and today he attends his uncle's funeral.'

She said, 'I see. Well, it doesn't matter,' and turned away defeatedly.

'Kyria Blake.' His voice was gentler. 'I think, maybe, it could matter very much. If you allow, I will drive you.'

'I can't ask you to do that.'

'You do not ask,' he said. 'I offer. Come.'

As they approached Villa Helios, Selena could see that the helicopter was out of the hangar and waiting on its pad.

She said, half to herself, 'It's too late.'

'No, no.' His tone was reassuring. 'See—Panayotis is still working on it, making checks. There is time.'

Eleni answered the door, red-eyed. 'Kyrios Alexis is not here,' she said in answer to Stelios's urgent question. 'He has gone to a meeting. I do not know when he will return.'

Selena stepped forward. 'Eleni—you're upset. What's happened? It's not—Penelope?'

'My daughter is in New York, with my lady, Madame Constantinou. When the house is closed up, we with Hara will be joining her there.'

'Closing the house? But I thought he was born here.'

'It is true, *thespinis*, and his mother will be deeply, deeply grieved that he should decide such a thing. She loves this house and hoped her grandchildren would be born here.' Eleni sighed. 'So many times she has said so.'

'Then why is he doing this?'

'Because he says his life is now in America. That there is nothing for him here.' She gave Selena a sorrowful look. 'He is a changed man, Kyria Blake.'

'Yes,' Selena said quietly. 'It would seem so.'

Stelios said, 'Shall I drive you back to the town, *thespinis*?'

'I suppose that would be best.' She turned back to

Eleni. 'Do you have any idea where Kyrios Alexis is having this meeting?'

'None, Kyria Blake. He took the Jeep and went.'

Her thoughts were whirling as she accompanied Stelios back to the car, trying to make sense of what she'd just heard. The house—closing. Alexis leaving Rhymnos for ever.

And at the same time, she found herself re-thinking everything that had happened between them.

Knowing that she needed to be totally honest with herself.

Admit she'd hoped that his coldness and contempt would be a kind of salvation for her, releasing her at last from the anguish of loving him. From the utter futility of hoping that—somehow—somewhere—there might still be a future for them both. Forcing her to accept that it was indeed—over.

Yet aware that here she was again, trapped in a maze of bewilderment, knowing there were now other questions that needed answers.

Realising that, without them, she would have no peace. Would be left wondering in some bleak wilderness.

She said under her breath, 'I have to find out. I have to…'

And suddenly she realised where Alexis would have gone.

Stelios was frankly unwilling to set her down at the track through the olive groves. 'Kyria Blake, this is a lonely place. Visit Apollo's temple if you wish, but I shall wait for you here.'

'There's no need,' she said as she got out of the car. 'I'm sure I shan't find it lonely at all.'

Difficult, she thought. Perhaps, in the end, impossible. But, for a while at least, not lonely.

'I shall still wait, *thespinis*,' he called after her.

'For half an hour, in case you are wrong.'

But, just as she'd known it would be, the Jeep was there, parked in the usual place.

She ran for most of the way and she was breathless when she finally reached the ridge and looked down into the precinct.

He was leaning against one of the pillars, a dark figure in the sunlight, his shoulders slumped as he stared towards the sea.

Motionless and solitary beyond belief, Selena thought, her heart twisting as she started down the slope.

Not there this time to make plans for the future, but to accept the defeats of the past.

And so lost in his thoughts that he was unaware of her approach until she said his name when he turned sharply, almost defensively.

'If you have come to say goodbye, it is not necessary. I thought my note made that clear.' His voice was harsh.

'It was perfectly clear,' Selena returned. 'But I decided I needed to clarify a few issues, too. Because I don't want us to part like this when there are still things that need to be said.'

'You wish me to apologise for the deal I proposed to you? Very well. The suggestion was shameful. Is that what you wish to hear?'

'No. Although I hated what you said, it was—almost understandable—considering what you were told.' She shook her head. 'I didn't know my aunt hated me so much.'

'You are saying she lied?'

'Yes,' she said. 'I am. I never contacted her when I returned to England. I suppose it was cowardice, but I couldn't bear to hear what I knew she'd say. And I'd always intended to leave what passed for home anyway.

'I moved to a larger town a few miles away where no one knew me. But one night, a few months later, an acquaintance of hers from Haylesford had dinner at the restaurant where I was working and told Aunt Nora that she'd seen me, that I looked well and appeared to have put on weight.

'So—she came to check. She sat at a table in the corner and watched me all evening. When I left, she was waiting outside—and she went on the attack.

'Oh, not physically,' she added quickly as Alexis took a step forward, his face darkening. 'Shouting—calling me names—saying that Millie and I were both disgusting little whores and worse. Totally out of control, using words I'd no idea she knew. Screaming that I'd disgraced her—damaged her good name for ever. That she would never be able to hold her head up in Haylesford again.' She tried to smile. 'She even mentioned nurturing vipers in her bosom.'

'I think the vipers would be most at risk,' he said. 'Go on.'

'There were some people passing and a man came over and asked me if I was all right or if I wanted the police to be called, and after that she calmed down a little. Began talking very reasonably and rationally about my pregnancy being still in the early stages, and how it could easily be terminated. That she would pay to have it done privately at some clinic in London and afterwards I could go back to university, complete my training and teach at her school, just as planned.'

She shuddered. 'In a way, the shouting was better.' She paused. 'When I told her I wouldn't consider abortion, and was going to have my baby, she became very quiet—very cold. Said I had twenty four hours to come to my senses, or she would make me sorry.

'That all contact between us would end. That I, and my bastard, could starve in the gutter for all she cared. And that she would change her will so that neither Millie nor I would ever see a penny of her money.' Again she attempted a smile. 'The ultimate threat.'

He said, 'But ignored.'

'Yes.' She sighed. 'Millie was furious when she found out and stopped speaking to me. She obviously thought I should have agreed to an abortion. But, now she's pregnant herself, she probably understands.'

'But I do not,' he said. 'If you had a choice, why wait until the child is born to be rid of him?'

She swallowed. 'It—it wasn't like that. After the birth, I—I was in a bad way. I had some kind of breakdown and the doctors and social workers felt I was in no fit state to look after myself, let alone a baby.

'And—and they were probably right. So I agreed to have him fostered until I could get on my feet again, find decent work and provide him with a proper home.

'But although I never saw or heard from Aunt Nora again, she must have been keeping tabs on me and discovered all this.'

She gave him a steady look. 'So when you arrived on her doorstep, she saw the perfect way to make me sorry. And did so.'

There was a silence, then: 'My God,' he said quietly. 'We are neither of us fortunate in our relations, Selene *mou*.' He paused. 'They are good people who are looking after Alexander?'

'The Talbots,' she said. 'Yes, good—and kind. Sticklers over visitation arrangements with me, but loving to him.' She paused. 'Maybe too much so because it will be hard for them when I take him back.'

She added, stumbling a little, 'But not as hard as it's been for me being without him all this time. Not able to watch him grow. Learn about things. Missing his first smile, first tooth, first step.'

She reached into her bag. 'Having to depend on things like this.' She handed him the photograph. 'I want you to have it. That's one of the reasons I'm here.'

He looked down at the photograph. He was very still but Selena saw a muscle move in his throat.

At last, he said quietly, 'You plan to take him back—to be with you.'

'I always did,' she said. 'I just had to prove, among other things, that I could find steady employment, which I now have and a decent place to live. I'm working on that.'

She hesitated, her heartbeat quickening. 'And when it happens, I'll have a deal to offer you. Access to your son. The right to visit him, and have him visit you wherever you happen to be living. To share in decisions about his education, well-being and future. To be his father.'

There was a long silence, then he turned away. He said, 'You are generous, but my answer must be—no.'

She was shaken to the core. 'You—don't want to see him—be with him? I—I don't understand.'

'When we first met, I told you how it was when my parents parted. How I was pulled between them, spending time with one, then the other. I remember seeing my mother cry when the car came for me and I had to say goodbye. Later, I realised she always feared that one day my father would decide to keep me. Demand sole custody.

'I swore then I would never do this to my child, or to his mother.'

'But—Alexis—you're not your father. I know I could trust you…'

'How do you know?' He swung back to face her, almost savagely. 'When I have kept the truth from you, believed insane lies about you, and offered you a bargain which was an obscene insult. Holy Mother, I hardly know myself any more.'

Her voice shook. 'I thought maybe we could put that behind us. Start again—for Alexander.'

'Tell me something.' He walked over to her, put his hands on her shoulders. Looked down on her, his gaze searching, intent. 'Why did you refuse to consider a termination of your pregnancy?'

'I—I don't know. It just seemed the wrong thing to do.' She tried to pull away. 'Let go of me, please.'

'No,' he said. 'That is an evasion. I insist the truth, or there is no hope for us.'

She said with sudden bitterness, 'Oh, you want your pound of flesh, don't you, Kyrios Constantinou? Then here's the truth—for better or worse and to hell with you!'

She swallowed, aware that slow tears were trickling down her face. 'Because all I could think of was that this baby—this tiny thing growing inside me was part of you. All I had left of you. And I could not bear to let that go.

'And when he was born, I wanted to die of unhappiness knowing that you would never know him—' her voice cracked '—or even hold him.'

Alexis's arms were round her, drawing her close. 'Don't cry,' he whispered into her hair. 'My beloved, my precious girl. I have you now, and I shall never let you go again.'

'But you're leaving,' she sobbed into his shoulder. 'Closing the house and going to America.'

'Because I could not bear to stay here without you. There wasn't one place without some memory of you to torment me.' He paused. 'I tried so hard to stop loving you, *agapi mou*. I told myself that I could take you— use you, then dismiss you without emotion. Make you suffer as I had done.

'Yet when you walked on to our balcony yesterday, I knew how impossible that was. That it would be like tearing the living heart out of my body. But I could only think how much I must have made you hate me.

'Today I came here only to say goodbye for the last

time. Instead, once again I began to think, and I realised that the name you had chosen for our son might mean you still cared a little. That I should not give up hope.'

'And I couldn't understand why you'd changed your mind—decided to let me go,' she said. 'And I needed to know. So I made the photograph my excuse to come and find you.'

'And, of course, you knew where I would be.'

'Yes, I knew.' She remembered something. 'Oh, God, Stelios is down on the road, waiting for me.'

'No,' he said. 'He will have gone by now, probably to the house to tell them I will be staying—after we return from England with our son.

'So will you break the rules, *matia mou*, and live with me until Father Stephanos can marry us?'

'Oh, I think so.' Her eyes were still misty, but her dawning smile was radiant. '*S'agapo*, Kyrios Alexis. *M'agapas?*'

'For as long as we both live, Kyria Selene.' He bent his head and began to kiss her slowly, even gently at first, the first touch of his mouth on hers a promise of future joy as they sank down to the grass, breathless and laughing, in each other's arms.

# EPILOGUE

It HAD BEEN a wonderful party, thought Selena, gazing dreamily through the window of the *saloni* into the gathering darkness.

There'd been tables in the gardens, groaning with food and drink, music, dancing, and what seemed to be the entire population of Rhymnos there to celebrate not just the first anniversary of her wedding to Alexis, but to drink to her health and happiness as she awaited the imminent birth of their second child.

There were exceptions, of course. Anna Papoulis had been one absentee and Kostas had been there only to deliver Millie and baby Dimitri to the festivities and collect them when it was over.

Although Alexis had allowed them to keep the tavern and stay, Kostas clearly still felt awkward around his powerful brother-in-law.

Millie, however, had no regrets about her mother-in-law's absence.

'Miserable old witch,' she'd muttered. 'Honestly, Lena, she's a nightmare. Every time I put Dimitri down for a nap, or if he makes the slightest sound, she's there, picking him out of his cot, so now he expects it and screams blue murder if he doesn't get instant attention.'

She'd looked across the courtyard to where Maria Constantinou, Alexis's mother, was sitting quietly with Xander on her silk-clad lap, the pair of them engrossed in the story she was reading to him. 'Really, you don't know how lucky you are.'

'On the contrary,' Selena said gently. 'I really, really do.'

She'd been a bag of nerves when Alexis first took her to America and the big rambling house on Long Island to meet his mother, only to find there'd been no need to worry as Madame Constantinou had come running to meet her, folding her into a scented embrace, and smiling through happy tears.

'At last,' she said. 'At last Alexis brings me a daughter to love.'

From the first, she'd been wonderful with Xander, unfazed by his small serious face and silent bewilderment at finding himself among strangers in such very different surroundings, coaxing him gently out of his shell and even persuading him to call her Ya-ya.

By the time they left Long Island, he had also come to accept that the tall young man who carried him on his shoulders, taught him with endless patience to swim and played ball with him as long as there were hours of daylight was 'Papa'.

And that 'Mama' was no longer the sad, quiet girl who had come each week to visit him in that other house which was already becoming a distant memory, but someone who sang and laughed and cuddled him as well as devising with Papa some wonderfully noisy games at bathtime.

Also that a visit to the kitchen at the house in America and here on Rhymnos was invariably rewarded with beaming smiles, petting and some freshly baked and delicious treat.

It had not taken long for him to see that he was on to a good thing, Selena reflected tenderly, and she was thankful for it. Thankful, too, that the Talbots' angry predictions that he would be traumatised if he left their care had been counterbalanced by the love that had surrounded him since the first day, turning his acceptance of his new life into a minor miracle.

She put a hand to her throat, gently fingering the exquisite diamond pendant that Alexis had fastened there only hours ago.

'A small memento, my dearest love, of a wonderful year,' he'd whispered, his lips caressing the nape of her neck. 'And of a perfect day.'

Their sole disagreement had been when Selena had suggested that if their new baby was a boy, they should follow custom and give him his grandfather's name Petros, which Alexis had firmly vetoed.

'He would see it as a sign of weakness,' he declared.

'But, darling, he's still your father,' Selena protested. 'No matter what he's done, you can't want this estrangement to last for ever. Besides,' she added, 'if we make the first move, then we occupy the moral high ground.'

'I doubt he knows such a thing exists,' he returned, his mouth twisting. 'And the baby will be a girl. My heart tells me so.'

A daughter who would be called Maria, a decision already mutually and joyfully arrived at, which had caused Madame Constantinou to weep with happiness.

And maybe it was still early days to talk of reconciliation between Alexis and his father, and she should wait and allow time to do its healing.

'So here you are, *agapi mou*.'

She jumped a little as her husband's voice reached her.

Alexis came to stand behind her, his arms sliding round her, his hands resting gently on the mound of her belly. 'I thought Nicos advised you to rest.'

'I wanted to unwind a little. Perhaps wait for the moon to rise.'

'We'll watch for it together. And then you must obey your doctor's orders.'

She said, keeping her voice casual, 'Is Nicos still here?'

'Yes, in the dining room drinking coffee with Mama. He said to tell you he asked Xander if he would prefer a sister or a brother, and our son replied he was hoping for a donkey.'

She giggled. 'He's talked about nothing else since the Stephanides foal was born.'

'Perhaps I should ask Takis if he would sell it. We can tell Xander it is a gift from the baby.' He paused. 'How is our little one?'

'Remarkably peaceful for a change. And seems to have changed position.' She relaxed against him. 'But my back has started to ache, so perhaps I've spent too much time on my feet. A massage later would be much appreciated.'

'It will be my pleasure.' He kissed the top of her head and they stood in silence for a while, simply content to be together, until Selena moved, sharply and uncomfortably.

'What is it?' Alexis was alerted instantly.

'My back. It's not just an ache any more.' She drew a deep breath. 'I think maybe I should go and lie down while you tell Nicos I seem to be having contractions. Quite quick ones. And warn Mama and Eleni, too.'

He said hoarsely, 'Ah, dear God,' and lifted her gently into his arms, carrying her swiftly and safely to their bedroom.

'This should not be happening here like this,' he said as he placed her on the bed, and helped her out of her pleated silk dress. 'I should have insisted that we stayed in America, where you would have the best of care.'

'As I shall get from Nicos.' She reached up and stroked his cheek lovingly. 'Because I want this baby born here, as you were, with everyone I love around me. It—it's important to me,' she added, her voice shaking a little.

'Ah, *matia mou*,' he said softly and bent and kissed her.

Left alone, Selena felt absurdly calm.

A perfect day, Alexis had called it, and this would be its unexpectedly perfect ending.

The contractions were getting stronger, and she made herself relax and breathe through them, each one bringing her a step closer to the moment when she would hold their new child in her arms.

A baby conceived one magical afternoon as the early autumn sun turned the temple columns to fire.

Our little Maria, she thought, or—maybe—it might be Petros, after all. I'll just have to trust Apollo the Healer. And she smiled.

\* \* \* \* \*

*If you enjoyed*
*THE INNOCENT'S SHAMEFUL SECRET,*
*why not explore these other*
SECRET HEIRS OF BILLIONAIRES *stories?*

*THE SHEIKH'S SECRET SON*
*by Maggie Cox*
*THE DESERT KING'S SECRET HEIR*
*by Annie West*
*DEMETRIOU DEMANDS HIS CHILD*
*by Kate Hewitt*
*THE SECRET TO MARRYING MARCHESI*
*by Amanda Cinelli*
*BRUNETTI'S SECRET SON*
*by Maya Blake*

*Available now!*

# MILLS & BOON®

# MODERN™

**POWER, PASSION AND IRRESISTIBLE TEMPTATION**

# MILLS & BOON®

## EXCLUSIVE EXTRACT

Ruthless Prince Adam Katsaros offers Belle a deal –
he'll release her father if she becomes his mistress!
Adam's gaze awakens a heated desire in Belle.
Her innocent beauty might redeem his royal
reputation – but can she tame the beast inside...

*Read on for a sneak preview of*
*THE PRINCE'S CAPTIVE VIRGIN*

"You really are kind of a beast," Belle said, standing up.
Adam caught her wrist, stopped her from leaving.

"And what bothers you most about that? The fact that
you would like to reform me, that you would like for your
time here to mean something and you are beginning to see
that it won't? Or is it the fact that you don't want to reform
me at all, and that you rather like me this way. Or at least,
your body likes me this way."

"Bodies make stupid decisions all the time. My father
wanted my mother, and she was a terrible, unloving person
who didn't even want her own daughter. So, forgive me if I
find this argument rather uncompelling. It doesn't make
you a good person, just because I enjoy kissing you. And
it doesn't make this something worth exploring."

She broke free of him and began to walk away, striding
down the hall, back toward her room. He pushed away
from the table, letting his chair fall to the floor, not caring
enough to right it as he followed after Belle.

He caught up to her, pivoting so that he was in front of
her. She took a step backward, then to the side, butting up
against the wall. Then, he caged her between his arms,

staring down at her. Her blue eyes were glittering, her breasts rising and falling rapidly with each breath.

"This is the only thing worth exploring. Not what could be, but what you have. The fire that burns between you and another person. For all you know, in the days since you've been here the entire world has fallen away. And if we were all that was left... Would you not regret missing out on the chance to see how hot we could burn?"

She shook her head. "But the world hasn't fallen away," she said, her trembling lips pale now, a complete contrast to the rich color they had been only moments ago. "It's still there. And whatever happens in here will have consequences out there. I will help you, Adam, but I'm not going to give you my body. I'm not going to destroy that life that I have out there to play games with you in here. You're a stranger to me, and you're going to remain a stranger to me. I can pretend. I can give you whatever you need when it comes to making a statement for your country. But beyond that? I can't."

Then, she turned and walked away, and this time, he let her go.

*Don't miss*
*THE PRINCE'S CAPTIVE VIRGIN*
by Maisey Yates

*The first part in her*
*ONCE UPON A SEDUCTION trilogy*

*Available June 2017*
www.millsandboon.co.uk

# Join Britain's BIGGEST Romance Book Club

- EXCLUSIVE offers every month

- FREE delivery direct to your door

- NEVER MISS a title

- EARN Bonus Book points

Call Customer Services
## 0844 844 1358*

or visit
## millsandboon.co.uk/subscription

# MILLS & BOON®
## are delighted to support
## World Book Night

*Georgie Lee*

*The Secret Marriage Pact*